Rise of Dragons – Book 4

Darkest Deception

G Clatworthy

Find more at www.gemmaclatworthy.com

Cover art by Sanjay Charlon (Beehive Illustrations)

Foreword

This story takes place in the Rise of Dragons universe; a world where magical and mundane beings coexist and dragons have recently been awoken.

The first three books in the Rise of Dragons series are told from the point of view of Amethyst Haernson, a half-dwarf jeweller who just wants a quiet life.

This book shows Special Agent Ruth Jones' point of view and is set just after the end of Book 2 and in parallel to Book 3. If you want to avoid spoilers of those two stories, take a break now to catch up! Otherwise, read on…and I've included Agent Jones' view of the end of Book 2 as Bonus Chapters at the end.

A special thank you to my amazing typo hunters, grammar gurus, and plot pickers who got this story to where it is today. You are awesome!

If you want to support Gemma, you can find her on patreon.com/G_Clatworthy for exclusive first reads of new stories. You can also join her newsletter for a free prequel to this series and follow Gemma on www.instagram.com/gemmaclatworthy, www.facebook.com/gemmaclatworthy or join the reader's group Gemma's book wyrms.

Prologue

I didn't like this mission. There was too much going on and too many civilians involved. It had started off well. I had been assigned the role of lead agent on a dragon taskforce. A massive responsibility and, if it went well, I could be looking at a big promotion. Not that I didn't enjoy running the Welsh branch of the Magical Liaison Office, but I wanted that next rung on the ladder. I hadn't sacrificed my personal and social life to not go the distance in my career.

After the first dragon had awoken earlier in the year and destroyed part of Cardiff Castle, the Magical Liaison Office had been trying to learn as much about them as possible. I had managed to recruit a leading dragon expert into the Office: Aloora Neebly or Dragonquest, her online handle and preferred moniker. The stubborn gnome had convinced me to bring along her friend and dragon survivor, Amethyst Haernson. A half-dwarf and talented metalsmith, I'd had her make some bespoke weapons for the team. I'd planned to keep her away from any action, but she had a knack for finding trouble. The elves had been on my case since they found out about the taskforce too. I'd had to accept one of them onto the team. I'd done my background checks and was happy with their proposal of a minor member of their royal family. Lorandir was a decent fighter and magic user specialising in healing magic; always a useful addition to a team.

Of course, I had my previous work partner and long-time friend from the London branch, Maxi, as our tech expert. I'd insisted he come along as soon as I'd been assigned the job. Dot, my trusted deputy, was our final member. She was a vampire but there was no one I'd rather have by my side if things went sideways.

Now we were at Stonehenge. In the middle of the Summer Solstice celebrations. And things had gone upside down, never mind sideways. Dragons had burst from the ground and attacked us before disappearing West and a member of my team had sold us out.

Chapter 1

I strode back to Madam Mim's picturesque cottage in the small town. She was there to answer the door before I'd lifted my hand to ring the antique bell pull. I forced myself to give her a polite nod. I didn't need to make an enemy of the powerful fae sorcerer. She offered me a small green bottle. I smiled as I recognised her own *Cure All.* I had forgotten about my injured arm in the excitement of dragons attacking us. I opened it. The combination of mint, aniseed and whisky stung my nose, but it worked. I rubbed a couple of drops onto my arm and the searing pain dulled to an ache. I took a swig for good measure. It was the closest I came to letting magic speed up my natural healing abilities and I was grateful for the release. I wasn't looking forward to what came next. I returned the bottle and set my face into hard lines. I couldn't let anyone know this was killing me inside.

I marched into the cosy living area. The team were sprawled out on various squashy chintz armchairs. I scanned the room until I saw who I wanted. Maxi was staring at a point on the wall. He was hugging himself, trying to look smaller. I felt for him. I quickly squashed that emotion down. He could be a damn traitor. I couldn't allow myself to think of him as anything other than that until I knew differently.

"You. Upstairs. I want answers," I stormed upstairs without waiting for him. I heard him trudging up the stairs. I waited and ushered him into the bedroom I was sharing with Dot. I closed the door behind him with a click.

He looked at me wide-eyed, his round cheeks making him look more youthful than usual. I gestured for him to sit down on one of the beds. He perched on the edge of a floral duvet cover, decorated with insects and fairies fluttering between large flowers.

I took a deep breath. I couldn't believe he'd betrayed us. I squashed down any sympathy I had for my friend and clenched my fists. I decided to play bad cop.

"What the hell was that at Stonehenge?"

"This wasn't supposed to happen…"

I lost my cool. I felt my fingers lengthening into claws. I had to let out some of my anger. I exploded, "It did happen! Start talking!"

Maxi swallowed several times and eyed me nervously, "It, well, the speakers, what,…then the sounds, yah…they didn't say it would…I trusted them!"

I pinched the bridge of my nose in frustration. I stalked off to the bathroom to get a glass of water. When I came back into the bedroom, I was in control again. I handed him the water and forced myself to speak more calmly, "Fill in those gaps for me Maxi."

He took a long drink. His eyes became less wild looking. He raked one hand through his hair. It stood on end like a mad professor's, contrasting oddly with his young face. He stared at his feet and began talking.

"They said I was the expert…you know I've been working with the equipment team, yah…they said they had a sound that would ensure the dragons would stay asleep…it would tap into their brainwaves. They've been testing it on wyrms, you know they have similarities to dragons…"

I curled my lip as he started into an enthusiastic lecture on species genealogy. He was too smart for his own good. Fortunately, he caught my look and got back to the point.

"...anyway, it was sanctioned so I thought it was fine. I was just following orders."

"Orders from who?"

"Whom…sorry," he took a nervous sip of water and carried on, "…I mean, the Director. He sanctioned the use of the sounds, told me you didn't need to be bothered with the details, that we were protecting the world…and I believed him."

He looked so sorry for himself that I had to stop myself from reaching out and patting his shoulder. Instead I walked to the window overlooking Mim's well-kept garden, considering. If what Maxi said was true then the desire to waken historic monsters wasn't just a cult fetish…it went to the top of the Magical Liaison Office.

The organisation dedicated to protecting the world and keeping the peace between magical and mundane. The organisation I worked for. The organisation I had dedicated myself to ever since I had been recruited, right after I'd left home. I had to know if he was telling the truth.

"I've got a problem here Maximillian Baskerville. If you're lying, it will go very badly for you when I call this in…but if you're telling the truth then it will still go badly for you because the Director isn't going to stick his neck out for you."

His mouth opened and closed, "I've been a complete fool."

"Yes. You have. Why wouldn't you tell me about this?"

"They said you didn't need to know details, that it was better to do it. I only got the new sound clips today on the drive over. There wasn't time, and, I trusted them."

"You said 'they', who else?"

He gave me the names of two people on the equipment team who had given him the sound files. They had buttered him up it sounded like, gained his trust and suckered him in. If he was telling the truth. I wanted to believe him more than anything, but I had to be smart. Either he was lying to me or the whole Office was one big lie.

"You stay here and write what you just told me down. Add in anything else that might help you." I needed a walk.

I marched into the garden, ignoring the herbs and other healing plants Mim kept in glazed pots. My ears picked up talking behind a screen of trailing roses. Their sweet scent filled my nose. Too sweet. I continued through the opening and into the other worldly forest set behind Madam Mim's cottage. The background magic pricked my skin. The entire taskforce was there. They stopped talking as they saw me. I felt my jaw clench.

"We're leaving after lunch," I turned on my heels and stalked back the way I'd come. Madam Mim held me back as the others passed.

"Don't be too hard on him."

I raised one eyebrow at her.

"I read his tea leaves, you know that. You didn't hear his fortune though…"

"Aren't you bound not to reveal the fortunes of others?" It was cruel but I hated mysteries and riddles.

"True," she regarded me carefully, "but I ask you to think who is really the betrayer and the betrayed here." She glided off towards the cottage to prepare lunch. I narrowed my eyes at her back and considered. I rubbed the back of my neck, swore and walked back behind the rose bushes. I wanted some privacy for the call I had to make.

I scrolled through my phone several times, deciding who to call. If Maxi was right, the Director was out. I could go above him to the powers that be…but if Maxi was lying I wouldn't win any friends doing that. Who of my colleagues did I trust? As I scrolled through my contacts, I lit upon a name. Damn it. My boss. Head of the London office. Technically I still reported into him, but I ran my own ship here in Wales. We'd had a few disagreements and I didn't like him…but…I'd worked with him for years.... I inhaled deeply and dialled the number.

"Jones."

"Hello Vass."

"What's going on in Wiltshire? I've got two separate clean-up teams called out and complaints coming in left, right and centre!" I could hear the shuffle of papers combined with noisy keyboard typing.

"Dragons."

He swore. "Looks like we were right about there being more."

I made an affirmative noise.

"Well, spit it out. You don't usually call me without wanting something."

"Are you alone?"

"I'm in my office. What is going on?"

I sighed, "I've got information. It's big…potentially."

In my mind's eye I could see him leaning back on his leather swivel chair, thinking. Then I heard the click of the glass door as he shut it. "Alright, I'm listening."

I filled him in. How he handled this would tell me if I could trust him.

He let out a low whistle while he thought, "This is big Jones…this is the closest I've come to getting anything concrete on the Director…"

"You knew?!"

"I had my suspicions. Nothing certain, just coincidences. We need to play this carefully, for all our sakes. He's a powerful man."

"You think I don't know that?!"

"Got a plan have you?"

I was silent. I didn't have a plan…yet.

"OK, why don't you meet me here in London or I can come to your Cardiff branch, it's due an inspection..."

"He put my entire team in danger! Plus two civilians I've got on this taskforce! I am not coming back into the office if what Maxi told me was true." My voice was rising. I fought to control my temper, "I can't work for a crooked organisation, it's too dangerous for everyone."

"I know you like the direct approach," he sounded derisive, "but we can't arrest him on the say so of one of your team. We have to do the work, build the case. Get a little thing called evidence."

I let his superior sarcasm pass. "What if I make the wrong call again? What if I trust the wrong person? It's too big a risk. I can't go back into the Office until I'm certain."

He let out a sigh of forced frustration, "Always making things difficult, hey Jones? You still want to work the case though?"

"Of course!"

I heard his fingers drum on the table as he thought it through. He was always better at planning ahead than me, "Alright, here's what you do: put in for a leave of absence. You haven't taken any holiday in the last year and a half.

I'll put it about that your latest mission has pushed you to the edge. No one's encountered dragons before, it won't be that much of a stretch for people to believe it." I frowned at the phone; patience was not my strong suit. He carried on, "You've got a competent deputy I assume?"

"Dot," I answered without hesitation. Before today I might have been torn between her and Maxi.

"OK, we'll put her in charge of the branch temporarily. Send Maxi back to London for a bit, reporting into me. I'll keep an eye on him in case he's involved and we'll dig around here."

"What am I meant to do?"

"First off, relax! Enjoy some time on your farm! I'm giving you paid leave here Jones! Second, while you're out, you're free. Freer than Maxi and me."

I took the hint. I could work the case without being confined by the Office's strict rules and protocols.

"I might need information from the internal databases…"

"I'll make sure you have access…I'll assign you some grunt work while you're on leave, to ease you back in. But be careful. Don't get caught by a data trail. If the Director finds out about any of this…"

"He won't."

"Good luck Jones."

He hung up. I didn't know whether I was happy that he was going to help or pissed that I'd agreed to do this covert operation. I definitely didn't like the idea of kicking my heels at my family's farm. I pinched the bridge of my nose, feeling a tension headache coming on.

Chapter 2

The news sounded loudly in the van as we drove back to Cardiff. I could almost be proud at the efficiency of the Magical Liaison Office for getting the releases out. A bomb scare for Stonehenge and gas leak for the Avebury stone circle, roadblocks in place. Neat and tidy.

I pressed one of the pre-programmed stations as we drove through one of said roadblocks and turned onto the main road. Nineties pop. I felt my shoulders relax as the upbeat music thrummed through the speakers. It reminded me of happier times, me and my Mum dancing in the kitchen. That was before. My shoulders instantly tensed up again. I winced as I changed gears, my injured arm jolting itself on the still gear stick.

I flipped my concentration back to the road and away from those painful memories. We joined the motorway at the Swindon junction and I was caught by another memory. Maxi and I on another Summer Solstice mission to investigate a magical seal. Good times. Now, he was subdued in the back. Dot was foregoing her daytime sleep to keep an eye on him. The others were all eyeing him warily too. Except Amethyst. She had fallen asleep and was drooling softly in one seat. I wished I could be that relaxed in cars, but I liked to be in control and got nauseous if I wasn't driving. A child facing backwards in the back of an estate car in front of me waved. I ignored them and pulled out to overtake the car loaded with suitcases and blow up beach toys.

Back in Cardiff, I dropped Aloora off outside the three-storey Victorian house on Miskin street where she lived. To my mind, it didn't fit her self-assigned moniker of 'Dragonquest' but hey, we all had to live somewhere. She was too new to the team to involve in the plan. Next stop was the main road outside Cardiff Castle. It still had a 'closed for renovation' sign hung on its formidable studded wooden gate. A leftover from the first dragon bursting into our world earlier this year. I could still smell the tang of sulphur…or maybe I was just imagining it. I pulled up sharply on a kerb in a no waiting zone. Amethyst and Lorandir got out and grabbed their bags from the back of the van. I didn't wait to see them off, instead I pulled out into traffic and headed for the Magical Liaison Office Cardiff Headquarters.

I turned into the side road just outside the city centre and pressed the garage door opening key inside the van. The pavement swung open, creating a ramp into the underground garage. I drove in, unconcerned about anyone paying us undue interest. The wards around the street made it completely uninteresting to mundane beings and the magical ones generally didn't want anything to do with our Office if they could help it. I drove us down the ramp into the sleek, modern garage and parked up next to my standard-issue grey Volvo. I slammed the van door as I got out.

"Hey, careful with Dan!"

"Dan?"

"Dan the van," Dot shrugged, "I thought he should have a name now he's magical."

I scowled. The fire rune the half-dwarf had managed to emblazon onto the floor had nearly blown the van up earlier on the trip. We'd have to do something to the fuel tank if we wanted to keep using its newfound magical abilities. I strode past the red punching bag hanging from the ceiling. I rubbed my neck. I could do with a good workout. It always helped me relieve tension and get my thoughts straight. But there was no time for that right now. I ignored the crashmats, targets and metal shelves with their various boxing gloves and weapons and carried on up a winding ramp to the first floor of our Office.

I heard Dot follow behind, an iron grip on Maxi's arm. At the top of the ramp, I jerked my head towards a holding room before heading to our main room. I paused in front of a maroon coloured wooden door with an ugly brass door knocker in the shape of a face.

"Face like thunder today Jones."

"At least I don't look like you."

"Harsh words. Maybe I'll just go to sleep and not let you in."

"Maybe I'll tear that knocker off your face and get you reassigned to the toilets!" I wasn't in the mood for Fred's banter today. Bloody door knockers, always wanting to let you know they've got the power.

"Alright, alright, tetchy! Manners don't cost anything you know! I've still got to see your pass or your eyeball. Your choice." Inasmuch as a brass door knocker could, he looked smug.

I pulled out my pass and held it up to his eyes. I considered slamming it into his brass face but decided against it. I needed him to let me in.

"Thank you kindly." The door swung open into the pentagon shaped room. I marched over to the kitchen behind a bookcase. I needed coffee. I pulled the black clothbound book, *Nom-Nomenclature of Supernatural Cuisine* – that was Dot's choice – and the panel hiding the kitchen swung open. I started the coffee machine for a double espresso and waited. As the coffee finished dripping into my angular mug, Dot entered. She carefully avoided meeting my eyes as she dug around in the fridge for her own personal drink supply. The metallic tang of blood assailed my nostrils as she heated it in the microwave. She always said it wasn't the same as the fresh stuff but better than drinking cold.

"You've got that look in your eyes," Dot tilted her head to one side as she looked at me.

"What look?"

"Like some bastard is going to pay for something and the poor sucker doesn't even know it yet." I didn't know I could be read so easily. She stirred her drink with a teaspoon before taking a sip, "What do you think?"

"Maxi's either a naïve fool or a genius criminal mastermind playing us for fools."

"Genius? Yes, I can see that. But criminal mastermind? He had to get contacts because he kept forgetting where he'd put his glasses!"

I let my mouth curl in a brief smile at the memory, "You don't think he intended to wake the dragons then?"

Dot shook her head, "No way. He's in total shock. But you know him better than I do."

"I thought I did," I sipped my own coffee.

"You've got a plan." It wasn't a question.

I nodded, "Can I trust you?" It was the wrong question to ask. The vampire's eyes instantly narrowed. She placed her mug down hard on the faux marble counter and strode out of the kitchen.

"Coming?" she yelled when she was half way across the main room.

I grinned and followed her. I knew what was coming next and I was ready for it. Dzrak, I needed it. We headed back down to the garage cum training area. She tugged off her chunky knit jumper and folded it onto a shelf. I shrugged off my linen suit jacket. We squared off on the blue crash mats, circling each other. I made the first move. Feinting left, I dived right and aimed a kick at her thigh. She dodged me easily. Damn vampires. She whirred out of the way in a blur. My instincts kicked in and I ducked to the side as she punched where my face had been. We were old adversaries on the mat. But she relied on her speed and strength over technique. We exchanged a series of blows and blocks, equally matched. Then she caught me on my injured arm. I winced at the sudden pain that spiralled through me and backed away. I wiped the sweat from my eyes. The vampire was still as cool as ever. Instead of blocking the next blow, I allowed Dot's leg to connect with my stomach. I grabbed her calf and bent to avoid being winded. I pulled hard, taking her off balance. I twisted, pushing her to the mat with my shoulder. It wasn't the most elegant move, but it worked. I felt her trying to get leverage beneath me to use her strength to push us both up. I shifted into my heavier lynx form and lay on her, pinning her shoulders with my large paws. Her eyes flashed. I closed my own. The rumours were true – a vampire's gaze could approach something like hypnosis. I was less susceptible than humans but didn't want to take the chance. Instead I laid my heavy chin on hers and looked straight ahead.

"Alright, alright, you win. Get your hairy chin off me. It itches!"

I purred in acknowledgement and shifted back. I got up first and offered her my hand. I pulled her up and filled her in.

"The Director huh?"

I nodded and felt my jaw clenching again. "I'm taking a break to work this case. You're in charge while I'm away," I held up my hand to stop her protest, "I need you to be my eyes and ears here. Aloora's great with dragon stuff but she's too new to the Office to understand the politics at play. Keep her busy, train her up, stay keen and keep me up to date with everything. This has to look natural and no one who knows me will believe I just left for vacation without checking in regularly." I pushed aside the thought that no one really knew me at the Office at all. I kept my private life to myself. Only a few people even knew I was a shifter.

"What about Maxi?"

"I'm sending him to London. Vass is going to babysit him."

"Is Vass trustworthy? I always thought he was a bureaucrat."

"He is…and a gigantic pain in the backside. But I think he's with us on this one. Said he's been investigating the Director for a while…just in case, I need you to reach out to your contacts in London. Keep an ear to the ground, subtle though."

"Understood," her face shifted from serious to a slight smirk, "and you never know, you might actually get to relax…maybe even meet someone…"

I narrowed my eyes and sent our standing punching bag careening towards her with a mighty throw. She caught it easily and leaned on it in the haughty, elegant manner of vampires and elves. She shot me a superior smile.

I turned and pulled on my suit jacket before rubbing the back of my neck. I had one last person to talk to before I left.

I entered the holding room with two double espressos in my hands. I placed one in front of Maxi and sat down opposite him in an uncomfortable metal chair.

"I'm so sorry…"

I had up my hand to interrupt him, "You messed up big time Maxi."

"I know," he hung his head miserably.

"We can't undo this."

No reply.

"I want to trust you…I'm giving you a chance."

"Anything! I'll do anything! I never meant for this to happen, I thought…"

"I know. You trusted the wrong people. So, I'm sending you back to London. You're going to be working with Vass. Keep him sweet but I want you to keep an eye out for anything suspicious and report back to me. Only me. You can contact me at the farm."

"You're going to the farm?" Maxi knew I practically lived at the office and barely went back to my family farmhouse.

I nodded. I didn't want to explain. "Dot's in the loop too. If you get into any trouble, call it in with her and me."

He met my eyes, "I truly am sorry. I will redeem myself and this organisation."

"Alright, alright, this isn't an Arthurian quest. Get your things and get on a train to London. Dot will escort you. Don't do anything else stupid and don't raise any suspicions. Stay away from the Director." I had a thought, after all he was our tech expert, "Before you go though…have a look at the van, it can set on fire now so probably not a good idea to have flammable fuel."

His eyes lit up as he focused on a problem that merged modern technology and magic, "Hmmm…I wonder, if I can calibrate the engine so it ran on a magically charged fuel cell…but would the type of magic matter? It's a dwarf rune causing the fire so…"

"I'll get you a pen and paper," I left him muttering to himself and running his hands one after another through his thick wild hair. By the time I got back with a pad of paper and a pen, his hair was sticking up all around his head. He grabbed the pen and immediately began scribbling. I left him to it and said my goodbyes to Dot.

I drove my grey Volvo back to my flat on the outskirts of the city, wincing every time I had to change gear with my injured arm. Slamming the door, I ran up the stairs, ignoring the lift. I considered my plans. It had seemed like such a good idea when I'd told Vass I'd go back to my family home. I poured myself a large glass of red wine, then I took a slug from the bottle. My shifter metabolism meant I wouldn't get drunk, but the buzz until the alcohol burned off helped take the sting out of being sent away. Even if I had agreed to go.

I decided to start packing. Keep moving. Get organised. I surveyed my wardrobe. My usual uniform of sharply tailored suits hung in colour order from wooden hangers. I selected a couple and wrapped them in a suit cover. I swore softly. I'd left my suitcase at the Office with the remains of the speakers in it. I folded the suits into my fake crocodile skin handbag. I'd have to hang them when I got there so they didn't get too wrinkled. I put in a pair of high-heeled stilettos for good measure. You never knew when you might need good shoes. I was glad my bag had been enchanted so it could carry everything I'd need.

I thought for a moment about my old home. A quaint country cottage set in a couple of acres of field. The nearest town was a fifteen minute drive away. Maybe crisp suits wouldn't be useful to me. I packed a couple of pairs of skinny jeans and plain tops as well as a shirt. My gym bag followed with all of my sports gear. I could at least up my fitness routine while I was away. I burrowed around in my basic training gear from my early days in the Office. I decided not to take my Office combat fatigues. My fingers lingered on my body armour. Being a shifter, I healed fast. No need to take that, it wasn't like I was going to be fighting anyone with silver tipped blades. I paused for a second before making sure my Fang Dagger and my crossbow were in there, along with a quiver full of bolts. Might as well do some training while I was gone. I was ready to go, but something made me stop.

I didn't want to go home. There. I admitted it. I didn't want to go back to the farm where my mother had died. My thoughts skittered away from that and back to work. Maybe Vass would change his mind about this whole thing. Yes. It could happen. Better if I stayed here tonight and gave him a few hours to think it through. He'd call me back tomorrow to check in and I didn't want to be miles away in the middle of nowhere. I changed quickly and went for a run around the city. I pounded the pavements hard. I was still frustrated about this whole situation.

Someone had betrayed the Office. And me. I was going to take a lot of pleasure in taking them in and hauling their ass up at a tribunal. A hot shower later and I decided it was definitely too late to head out today. Instead, I ordered a take-away and binged on noodles while I watched a boxset. I'd go tomorrow.

Chapter 3

Tomorrow came with no call from Vass telling me to come back into the office. I wasted the morning cleaning my flat. Aloora texted me to say she believed Maxi and would like him to be part of the team again. I ignored her. Still no call from Vass. I tried to stare down my phone. It stayed resolutely silent. I gave up. Time to face this. I rolled my shoulder. My injured arm was still a little achy, but it was better than yesterday. I got into the car, set my bag on the passenger seat, where it contrasted with the dull fabric and started driving.

I drove through winding roads, ignoring the lush green countryside as I headed for the farm. Not so much a farm as a farmhouse with a couple of outbuildings and a bit of land. I tapped the steering wheel impatiently as I got stuck behind tractors and lorries that were enjoying slowing the scant traffic as I got further into the Welsh countryside. I inwardly cursed my mother for picking the most rural place she could find. I immediately felt guilty. I pushed those feelings down. I tried to avoid thinking about my parents. I turned on the radio and cheerful nineties pop music blasted through the speakers. My mouth formed into a smile. Those tunes always cheered me up.

Eventually I pulled off the main road and onto a dirt track that led to the farm. The rusty gate was hanging wide open. Another pang of guilt. I hadn't done any upkeep on the place in years. It showed. Wildflowers and overgrown grass had taken over the gravel driveway. Trees had grown wildly and their branches were too close to the house. I forced the car through the long stems, carving a path to the house. I pulled up outside. The farmhouse itself looked dismal. A faded shutter hung precariously from a single hinge. Another had fallen completely off. Single pane windows were covered with dirt. A wisteria plant had grown out of control and, along with the ivy, was covering half of the house. I glanced around at the outbuildings. An old barn was missing half its roof. A rusty ride on lawnmower sat next to something covered by a tarpaulin. I'd check that out later.

I decided to face the house first. The key stuck in the lock. I jiggled it a few times before it gave way and opened onto a dark hallway. I stepped inside and flicked the switch. Nothing. I turned on the torch on my phone. Dust lined the floor. I left footprints as I entered further inside. The furniture was exactly as I remembered it, albeit neglected and dirty. A window in the kitchen had broken leaving it open to the elements. I turned my phone light off as the golden glow of evening sun shone into the room. Judging by the puddle on the Welsh flagstone floor, it had been broken a while. A scrabbling sounded. I paused, on alert. I edged forward towards the chimney. With a burst of speed a jackdaw exploded out of the range cooker. It cawed angrily as it flew past me and out of the broken window. The tang of droppings hit my nose. Combined with the dust, it made me sneeze. Great. I took a few photos on my phone. For some reason, I wanted to record the decay. As if I didn't feel guilty enough about leaving this place. Besides, Dot would find the idea of me living here hilarious. I had a minimalist aesthetic to my modern flat and on my desk at work.

I ventured upstairs. The floorboards creaked under my tread. I flashed my phone's torch into the main room. Mum's room. Too painful. I kept going, seeking out my old room towards the back of the house. I paused at the threshold. A tree branch had forced its way in through the window. More scrabbling. A small brown bird fluttered out. A squirrel, braver than its feathered companion, looked me in the eye. It cocked its head to one side and gave an aggressive chirp, its tail bristling behind it. I pinched the bridge of my nose and sighed loudly. It wasn't worth it Jones. Instead I shone my phone directly at it and snapped a picture. With an angry chattering, it scampered off. I took in the rest of the room. My bed was directly under the large tree branch, covered in bird's mess and squirrel poo. The bedding had been shredded for use in something's nest. The faded posters of pop princesses and boy bands reminded me of foolish daydreams. Of a time when I thought anything was possible. I turned away. Those days were gone. A draught made me look up. A small patch of sky was visible through the roof. I stepped forward to take a closer look. The wooden floorboards were spongy under my feet. A large brown patch around the hole in the ceiling suggested rain had been getting in for a while. I stepped backwards, unwilling to trust my weight on the decaying floor for too long.

I descended slowly. Would I have to spend the night in the car? I'd camped out in worse places over the years. My eyes lit on another outbuilding. It looked in a lot better shape. Mum had started converting it when she was alive. Double glazing and a cheerfully painted door were testament to her efforts. I smiled briefly as I remembered painting it together, talking about our plans to rent it out. Better times. I mounted the iron steps to the barn style door and unlocked it. It had the same musty smell of a disused building but the years had been kinder. No wildlife had intruded and no trees had burst in. I checked in the cupboards. Neat white crockery was stacked carefully. There were a couple of boxes of teabags and a sealed jar of coffee granules. I dug around until I found the kettle. A bright red modern thing that somehow looked old. Retro style I guess you'd describe it as. Mum always had an eye for what would look good. I tried the tap. The water was working. I let it run for a minute to clear the pipes and made myself a cup of tea. Black. I rooted around in another rustic style cupboard and was rewarded with bedding. It was musty but clean. I made the bed, thankful Mum had invested in fitted sheets. My stomach rumbled. I checked the time on my phone. If I remembered anything about living in rural Wales, any shops would be shut by now. I walked back to the car to dig out my mock crocodile handbag and fumbled in it for a cereal bar. The problem with having an enchanted handbag is that it can be hard to find things. After a few minutes, my hand grasped the wrapper and I pulled it free with a gleam of triumph. I took it and my bag back to my new home and ate it slowly while I gazed at the setting sun.

The fields seemed tinged with gold and if I closed my eyes, I could almost imagine I was a teenager again. I couldn't wait to leave this place…even before. Before Mum had got cancer and I'd watched her get weaker and weaker, spending my late teens and early twenties caring for her until finally she breathed her last. That was when I'd locked the door and moved to London, hoping I could lose myself in work in the big city. It had worked. Until now. Now I was being forced to stay here, out of the way, where everything reminded me of her and how I'd lost all my family. I pushed myself up. I needed to run off these feelings. I found my exercise gear and headed out. I decided to do laps of the land we…I... owned today and trusted to my supernatural senses to keep me from tripping on hidden hazards in the long grass. The stems whipped my thighs as I ploughed through. I relished the stinging sensation and picked up my pace. Why hadn't I just sold this place? Deep down, I knew the answer. It was all I had left of her. I couldn't let that go, even if I didn't want to be here. I pushed those thoughts away and focused on the run. After an hour, I let myself back into the small flat with satisfaction. I lay on the bed and fell instantly to sleep.

I woke early. A watery sun peeped through one of the windows. I'd forgotten to close the curtains. I poured myself a cup of strong black coffee. The granules were long past their best and I gagged at the bitter taste. I dug out another emergency cereal bar from my bag. I needed to do some shopping. I checked the time. Run first. This time I decided to leave the farm. I vaulted over a stile onto a familiar footpath and set into a steady pace. In the calm of the countryside I allowed the sounds and smells to wash over me like I had when I was younger and needed time away. So different to the city. Birdsong filled the air. Grass mixed with meadow flowers and sweet blackberries filled my nose. I caught a whiff of rain in the air. I decided to run around the next field before heading back. I followed the ancient footpath and the farmland gave way to a more open hill as the path inclined upwards. A few sheep glanced my way before continuing to munch on the close cropped grass. A couple of low rocks jutted from the ground.

I smelled the man and his dog before I saw them. Too late to change direction and nowhere to hide on the exposed hillside.

"Enjoying an early morning run is it?"

I smiled politely. He stood in the path. I slowed down to avoid mowing into him. The dog whined and strained on its lead. Dogs either loved me or hated me. I always put it down to the shifter smell. I slowed to pat its soft head.

"You on holiday?"

"Something like that."

"Where you staying then? Only place round here is the old Jones house."

I nodded vaguely and made a show of checking my watch, "Got to keep going." I jogged on the spot to reinforce my words before setting off again. I circled back around the field, dodging the piles of sheep poo and managed to avoid seeing the dog-walker again as I jumped another gate and ran along the edge of a field. A tractor was bimbling along in parallel to me. I saw the driver give me a wave and I nodded in return before heading back into my own land. I had a quick shower before turning my car around and driving into the nearest town.

I parked up and looked along the familiar high street. The aroma of freshly baked bread filled the air, making my mouth water. I headed to the bakery first. As I asked for a couple of baguettes, the middle aged lady behind the counter stared at me. She smelled familiar behind the flour and yeast scents. One of my old classmates. My best friend in a former life.

"I can't help thinking I know you from somewhere…"

I forced myself to smile, but shrugged in reply. I didn't want to make a connection with the past. I was here to do a job nothing more. I handed over a few coins and turned to the door.

"Ruthy? Is that you?" An elderly lady stepped into the shop. I forced back a sigh. I had hoped not to be recognised. My mistake for coming to the closest town. I turned to look at the lady. A wave of nostalgia washed over me. Mrs Hillson. I had spent many afternoons at her house after school, avoiding going to my own home after Mum and I had argued.

"You haven't aged a day deary!"

"Ruth?! That's how I know you then. You remember," she tapped herself on her chest, "it's me…Claire."

"Of course, wow, that's…"

"Mum, isn't that amazing – it's Ruth!" The grey-haired lady nodded along in agreement. "Are you back then?"

"For a while."

"Well you'll come over to our place for dinner one evening. It'll be like old times! I can even make those turkey dinosaurs you used to like!"

"Mum, we're not ten!"

My smile was becoming more strained, “I have to get going…” I edged towards the door, the baguettes tucked under one arm.

“Come over tonight, you remember the address?” Claire’s mum grasped my wrist. It was clear I wasn’t getting out of there without agreeing. I nodded. I got out of the bakery and crossed the street. Claire caught up to me, her apron strings whipping in the breeze. She shoved a piece of paper in my hand.

“It’s good to see you,” she smiled and headed back to her shop. I glanced down at the paper. Her phone number. Great. Now I didn’t have an excuse. With an inward groan, I pushed open the door to a small supermarket. The bell above the door rang in my ear. I shivered as the cold from the open fridges storing drinks and sandwiches hit me.

The lady behind the counter eyed me as I grabbed a wire shopping basket and selected some food. I didn’t even know if the fridge was working so I only got enough to last me until tomorrow morning. I’d have to get the electricity sorted today. I was getting annoyed at the stare from the counter so grabbed the first shower gel and soap I could see, along with every sort of cleaning product they had. I dumped the basket on her counter and watched as she efficiently scanned it all through. She seemed unable to stop herself from commenting on every item and I nodded along, focusing on a point behind her shoulder. Eventually she asked me a question I had to reply to.

“Do you want a bag for that?”

I looked down. I had been planning to shove everything into my enchanted handbag, but that would draw more attention to me. “Please.”

The lady added a canvas bag to my shopping. She wasn't a fool. That was the most expensive bag she could have given me, the name of the shop in large letters on one side providing free advertising for her. I decided not to argue. She watched me with friendly brown eyes as I packed everything in.

"That's a pretty bracelet."

I immediately moved my arm so my top covered the jewelled cuff. I felt exposed. I didn't want to draw too much attention to myself but my magic dampener bracelet came in handy when I didn't want other magic users to recognise my shifter magic. At least I told myself that's why I wore it all the time. Aware that the pause had gone on too long, I replied, "My mother gave it to me."

A pang of emotion rang through me as I mentioned Mum. She had given it to me to keep me safe, as a reminder that there were those who would hunt our kind down… I pulled myself back to the moment in time to see the old lady smile. She didn't seem to notice my introspection, "Staying at the old Jones place are you?"

I narrowed my eyes at her. She laughed, "My husband was doing the fields this morning, said he saw someone going into the old farm."

I smiled at the small town gossip network in full force. If only all mysteries were so easy to solve.

"So now, you'll be wanting a builder there," I tried to protest but she slotted a business card into my bag. "My son's one of the honest ones. He'll help you out, you want to be careful of some of the others round here. Bloody cowboys." Her voice turned bitter. I didn't want to be embroiled in a local saga of cowboy builders so thanked her and exited quickly.

One last stop. I climbed back into my car and shoved the groceries on the passenger seat. I thudded the car into first gear forcefully. I was upset and unnerved at being recognised and forced into dinner tomorrow. I pulled out aggressively onto the empty street and drove to the garage. During the short journey I berated myself. What did I expect coming back to this place? Of course someone would recognise me. My smart city suits and tall stature stuck out in the small town. And it wasn't like I'd blended in even when I was younger. I filled up the car and a couple of canisters with diesel for good measure. I inwardly hoped I'd picked the right fuel for the generator back home. The liquid I remembered pouring into the generator certainly smelled as pungent as diesel. I crinkled my nose in disgust at the strong smell. I paid and walked across the forecourt back to my car. A van had pulled up. A ladder was strapped to the top and it stank of cigarette smoke. I caught the nudges of two blokes in their thirties eyeing me. I squared my shoulders and forced myself to keep going.

"Here! You must be the newcomer at the Jones place." News travelled fast. I ignored them. The one with dirty blonde hair walked over and leaned on the bonnet of my car. His chequered flannel shirt was too small for the beer belly he was growing.

"Just don't hang around too long…we don't take kindly to your sort here."

I froze. Did they know I was a shifter? My hand went reflexively to my golden magic dampening cuff. I didn't sense any magic from them. How could they possibly sense me? I looked again at my copper coloured hand touching my cuff. Of course. They were referring to my skin colour, unusual in these parts. Just your run of the mill idiots who didn't like outsiders. The thought was mildly comforting compared to other possibilities. Like hunting down shifters for sport…I jerked my mind away from that road quickly. I opened the car door and got in. They weren't the ones who'd killed my Dad and they weren't worth my time.

"Watch out for mountain lions, rumour has it there are some out there in the hills," the blonde one drew his fingers in lazy circles through the dust on my car, "I don't normally like outsiders but I could keep you company if you like…get inside...her." He shot his friend a grin.

Great. Perverts too.

"Someone died in that house you know!" The one at the van called out to me, oblivious to his friend's cunning grin. He adjusted his peaked cap. The logo on it read *Body Inspector*. Classy.

I slammed the car door and revved the engine. I stared at the blonde one. My amber eyes meeting his grey-blue ones. His eyes widened in shock as I allowed the car to start moving forward. He moved quickly to one side, thumping the bonnet as he did so. He wasn't strong enough to even dent it. I drove off, eyeing him in the mirror. I shook my head. The old rumour about mountain lions was still strong then. I could almost smile. Mum and I had started that rumour with our moonlit runs in shifter form across the hilltops.

Back at the house, it had begun to rain. I found the generator at the back of the house in the old coal shed. The tin roof was intact. I poured the diesel into the generator and turned it on. The ancient machine choked into life, filling the air with an oily tang. I went inside and flicked on a light switch. It sputtered into life and then winked out. The bulb was dead. No matter, I was staying in the outbuilding anyway. I strode over to the smaller house and tried the switch. The light stayed on. Good. A slight hum from the small under-counter fridge told me that was working too. I bent down to check it out. A sticky stain on one of the shelves made me pause.

The hairs on the back of my neck prickled up. I wasn't alone. Someone was watching me. I weighed my options. My weapons were in my handbag. In the car. I was good at hand to hand combat…or I could shift. But if whoever was watching me was mundane, that would lead to more problems. I turned slowly, trying to make it seem natural. No one there. I moved to the door and scented the air. The fumes from the generator were too raw in my nose. I couldn't smell anything. I turned my head a few times. All I could hear was the swishing of grass, the pattering of the rain and birdsong. I would have heard someone coming along the gravel drive I was sure. The feeling passed but I was on edge. Still uneasy, I went back to the car to grab my supplies and my bag.

Chapter 4

To distract me from the unnerving sense that there was someone else on the farm with me, I rang the shopkeeper's son and arranged for him to give me a quote for some work. I was confident I could do a lot with my shifter strength and I had time to kill, but I needed access to tools and a builder's yard and there was structural damage to the house that I had no idea how to assess. Next was trying to sort some internet connection out here. The company said it would take a couple of weeks and no amount of urgency or complaining on my part could change that. I even pointed out that the only place inside I could get signal on my mobile was the corner of the bedroom. No change. I hung up in annoyance.

Needing to clear my frustrated energy, I cleaned. The acrid chemical smells of the cleaning products stung my nose and throat. I opened a window and shoved a towel on the sill to stop the rain making its way in. That was better. I scrubbed years of accumulated dust away. I chased spiders out of the door into the summer shower. I swept up the carcasses of flies, long dead and dried out. Anything to stop my thoughts dwelling on my childhood. I snapped a few photos of the aftermath of my cleaning. The place looked bright and airy.

The rain stopped ten minutes before my appointment with the builder. He arrived right on time. I appreciated punctuality. I let his van roll up the grass my own car had flattened. I saw him looking up at the farmhouse, appraising it. Whatever figure he had in his mind would only go up when he saw the state of the inside.

He stepped out of the van and looked around. That was my cue. I dusted my hands off and stepped outside. Builders dust and sawdust filled my nose. Honest working smells. I smiled and held out my hand. "Sam?"

He smiled back and took it, a little surprised at the strength of my grip. "The very same! No wonder you gave me a call! This place needs a bit of work and no mistake."

"I want to do as much as I can myself."

"Sure," he nodded with respect as he took in my toned arms and muscled shoulders in my workout gear. I hadn't wanted to dirty any of my suits while I was cleaning. "Well, let's see what we've got then shall we."

I led him inside. He took a stubby pencil from behind his ear and made notes as I listed the things I knew about. The jackdaw in the kitchen chimney cawed menacingly as we talked about clearing its nest. Upstairs, he let out a tuneless whistle as he saw the tree branch taking over my old bedroom.

“I haven’t seen anything like that before, I’ll tell you,” he made to step in. I gripped his forearm.

“I’m not sure the floorboards are safe,” I answered his puzzled expression as I released his arm.

He bent down and pressed the wooden floor with his thumb. The wood dented at the slight pressure and water pooled on top. He scribbled furiously in his small notepad then looked up at the ceiling. “There’s your problem!”

I followed his gaze to the patch of cloudy sky peeping through the roof and nodded glumly. He let himself into the attic and shone a torch around. “The felt’s gone up here, and looks like it’s been exposed for a while. I’ll have to have the whole roof off.”

“Can’t you just patch the hole? Retile that bit?”

He shook his head as he descended the ladder, “Sorry love, it doesn’t work like that. Anything else I should know about?”

I gazed around and shook my head, letting the ‘love’ endearment go. For now. We walked down the stairs in silence and I let him out.

“It’ll look lovely once it’s done.”

I appreciated the effort to cheer me up but I wanted facts and figures, “What’s the damage? Give me a ballpark.”

He rubbed the back of his neck and sucked in a breath of air. Never a good sign from a builder. “Look, I want to do a proper quote on this…” I opened my mouth to press him and he carried on, “…but it’s not going to be below thirty grand…the roof alone will be about twenty I should think if I've got to get beams replaced as well."

That figure was more than all my savings. "Right, well thanks for coming out. Send me through a full quote and we'll see."

"Sure, have a good day then." I watched him leave in the van. I didn't doubt that he had given me an honest figure but that was a lot of money. I checked the time. Good. I still had time for a shower before heading over to Mrs Hillson's place for dinner.

I was just drying myself off when I felt it again. The prickle of eyes watching me. I stared through the window. Nothing. I heard a small footstep. Someone was moving carefully. I made my way to the small kitchen and fished in my handbag. My hand closed on the standard issue crossbow. I always kept it loaded. I held it up, sighting along it as I tried to pinpoint where the noise had come from. My other hand gripped the old towel tightly around my body. A crash of crockery to my right. I whirled and shot the crossbow instinctively. A blur of movement. My eyes caught up with my reflexes. A mug had fallen off the counter and smashed on the hard stone floor. The crossbow bolt was stuck in one of the ancient beams. Someone was in the house. How had they got past me?

The hairs on my neck stood up…what if it was a something? I shut the door with a click.

They weren't getting out. I reloaded my crossbow carefully. I considered switching to one of the carving knives in a drawer but if I could get an advantage with the bow, I'd take it. I padded softly through the kitchen. I knew I wasn't making a sound. I scanned the open plan living area. Nothing. I pulled the window shut. Now there was no way out. Bedroom then. I carried on. I inhaled deeply at the bedroom door. I burst through, scanning the room as I'd been taught in my training. Nothing. I frowned, puzzled. What the dzrak was going on? My eyes fell on the bed. The bed with a gap underneath. A gap large enough for someone to hide under. I narrowed my eyes.

"I know you're under the bed. Come out now, slowly, or it will be worse for you."

No reply. With a sigh, I crouched and aimed. A pathetic mew came back. My eyes focused on the small shape curled under the bed. A cat. I dropped my crossbow.

"Come here then you silly thing. You gave me a fright, you know that," I softened my voice but the cat stayed where it was. "Right, I don't have time for this. You stay there then and I'll be back soon, then we can talk." Two yellow eyes blinked in response.

Muttering to myself about how stupid I was, I got ready. My usual smart suits weren't going to endear me to anyone here, so I picked out a pair of fitted jeans and a t-shirt with a jacket. At least I had brought some casual clothes with me. I didn't really need them in the city. I was either at work or working out. Sad really, if you thought about it, so I didn't. I set out a bowl of water for the cat and picked up the bottle of red wine I had bought at the small supermarket before heading out.

Chapter 5

Despite having practically lived round Claire's house while I was at school, I took a wrong turn. There weren't a lot of places to turn around so I was ten minutes late when I finally got there. As I stared up at the stone house, I was embarrassed. I'd been so keen to get out of the town and put distance between the bad memories, that I'd avoided the good things too. I hadn't stayed in touch with anyone. Not even my former best friend. I shook myself mentally and forced on a smile that I hoped looked genuine before pressing the doorbell. Mrs Hillson's small form appeared behind the glazed door.

"Come in, come in child, you'll catch your death out there."

It was late summertime and the earlier rain shower had blown itself out but Mrs Hillson was always concerned about her children. I offered her the wine, which she took with a smile before bustling back towards the kitchen. I followed her. Claire was chopping vegetables on the counter.

“Let me help,” I offered awkwardly. Mrs Hillson beamed and found me a sharp knife. Without thinking, I twirled it in my hand before starting on some carrots.

“Wow, that’s…something else.”

I caught the glances between Claire and her mother. “Force of habit, sorry,” I stared at the wonky carrot in front of me as I cut it into neat slices.

“So, what are you up to nowadays? I don’t think I’ve seen you in, oh, must be fifteen years?”

“It’s been a long time,” I agreed.

“And? What are you doing? I always said you’d be running a company by the time you were thirty! You were always such a good girl, got your grades…” Claire’s mum shot her a meaningful look.

“I run a government office actually, it’s pretty bureaucratic though, a lot of paperwork, nothing like running a bakery!” I deflected away. I didn’t need to bring the magic part of my work into their lives.

“Yes Mum, exactly, I don’t need bits of paper to tell me how to run my business!”

“I never understood how you two were so different and yet thick as thieves…” Mrs Hillson shook her head as she pointed a wooden spoon at us, “Now, leave me be while I finish up here. I’ll call you in when it’s ready.”

Claire made a face behind her mum’s back and led the way to the front room. It was the same mauve colour it had been painted twenty years ago, when Mrs Hillson had gone through a DIY phase. I caught a glance of both of us in the hallway mirror as we passed. We made a strange pair. Me: tall and dark with my copper skin and black hair, Claire: short, curvy and blonde with blue eyes to match. We were different at school too. I was quiet, kept to myself, got good grades. Claire was confident, the class clown.

"You look like you're thinking hard!" she pulled me from my thoughts.

"I was just thinking…do you remember the day we met?"

She laughed, "Of course! That bully Billy was pulling your pigtails, but you weren't crying, you were looking at him like you could kill him if you wanted to but were choosing not to! I couldn't stand it!"

"You marched right over and punched him in the stomach before leading me away to redo my hair!"

"I always did have a good right hook! I loved your hair, so sleek and dark, not like my curly mop! How much time did we spend trying to copy the looks of our favourite popstars?"

I laughed, "Too long!"

"So tell me, any men in your life? Any kids?"

"Not for me, it's all work, work, work. You?"

"I'm married now," she held up her hand showing off her diamond engagement ring and a plain band beneath it, "five years me and Sam have been married. He's got the twins tonight. I told him we'd be staying up all night, just like old times!"

“Not Sam the bricks?!” I used the old nickname we’d given our classmate as he was constantly creating constructions with building bricks.

“The very same! I always thought he had a crush on you, but he finally got up the nerve to ask me out and here we are. I’m now Mrs Bricks, well actually Mrs Lewis. I tried to send you an invite, but no one had your address and I tried looking you up on social media but I couldn’t find you…” she was twisting her ring on her finger and staring at it.

I reached over, “I’m sorry Claire…it’s just, after Mum…it was too painful, I had to go…”

“I know that, but, you could have stayed in touch. You were my best friend here, then you were gone. I wanted to talk to you. I was alone too you know.” There was more than a hint of reproach in her voice.

“I really am sorry.”

Claire placed her hand over mine. She seemed about to say something then we heard her mum bellow down the hall. “Let’s go eat,” she said and led me back to the kitchen and through to the conservatory, where a round table was already laid.

My mouth was already watering. I thought back fondly to breaded turkey dinosaurs and oven cooked chips after school. I looked down at the plates. This evening Mrs Hillson had provided the adult equivalent: chicken kiev with buttered potatoes and steamed vegetables. I cut into the crispy chicken and allowed the garlic sauce inside to flow onto the plate. I wasn’t normally a fan of butter, but it added a richness to the meal.

"This is really good, thank you."

"Not a worry, love. How's the old house looking then? I haven't been up to see it since…well, yes…"

I interrupted before she finished that sentence. I didn't really want to talk about Mum. "It's pretty run down actually. There's a tree in one of the rooms and the roof needs redoing."

"Ah no, that's too bad. Are you going to do it up?"

"I'm going to try…I had one estimate today, I'm going to need to do a lot of the work myself."

"Who did you have out to look at it?" Claire was curious.

"Sam. He's the son of the lady in the supermarket."

They both nodded. Mrs Hillson said, "He's the best one around, you can trust him. He did my conservatory."

"And he's my husband!"

I blinked in surprise. I was annoyed I hadn't made the connection earlier, how many Sam's were there in this small town. I gave Claire's hand a squeeze as I looked around the room we were in. It was tastefully done with a small log burner tucked into one corner meaning the family could use it all through the year. I didn't know much about building but it looked good.

"Whatever you do, don't hire Billy Biggels and his mate. Right cowboys they are! Always smoking those cigarettes. I swear they'd do anything for some cash, goodness knows how they're still in business." Mrs Hillson shook her head disapprovingly.

“Weren’t they on that show about crooked builders a few years ago?”

I smiled along as they began talking about TV shows I’d never seen. Eventually the talk got back around to the farm.

“Still, it’s a shame you can’t rent out one of the buildings. Mary always talked about doing that, earning some money from the place. That would help pay for repairs.”

I froze. Hearing Mum’s name without being ready for it was like taking an ice cold shower. I reached for my glass of wine, covering up the emotions. Inwardly I chastised myself. I was back at the place where I’d grown up. A place where people knew each other and their goings on. Of course her name would be mentioned. I should have been ready. Mrs Hillson didn’t seem to have noticed my pause as I took a long swig of drink.

“What’s that?”

“I said it’s a shame you can’t rent out the guest house there.”

I frowned. Now that I wasn’t focusing on the throwaway mention of Mum’s name, the idea had merit. “That’s a good idea. The guest house is in decent shape…”

The conversation turned to other holiday homes in the area and then to holidays in the sun. I nodded along, contributing very little as I allowed the comforting conversation to wash over me. This could be part of the answer. I didn’t like the idea of sharing my space but I needed the money. I’d been planning to stay in the guest house but I could easily camp out in the main house. By the time I left, my head was swirling with thoughts about how much I could charge. I sat in my car for a few minutes to use the phone signal in town to look up a few similar places in rural Wales. They were charging hundreds a week in the summer and all seemed to be booked up. Impetuously I created an account on a popular site and uploaded the after pictures of the small guest house, set the availability for the rest of the year and added a high price per week. Humming along to a familiar nineties tune on the radio, I set off back home.

When I let myself into the outbuilding, the cat was curled up on the small sofa bed. A dark spot on the cream cushions. I stared at her, wondering what to do. She met my gaze with her yellow eyes then settled her head back down on her paws. She'd clearly decided to stay. She looked lean but not unhealthy. Her coat was a bit shabby. I wondered briefly about her life then decided that I had enough to think about without stray cats taking up my mental energy.

Chapter 6

I woke before dawn to a soft rumbling vibrating in my stomach. I looked down and found the small cat curled up next to me.

"Oh no, this isn't going to fly. We need to set some boundaries," I undermined my own words by stroking her soft head. Looks like she was comfortable here. I watched her quietly for a minute. She was white with patches of tabby fur picked out on her flank and paws. One large black patch covered one eye.

I left the bed and pulled on my workout gear. I couldn't face the awful coffee so I drank a glass of water as I considered. It was early morning. The sun wasn't up…I made my decision. The cat wound her way around my feet. I ushered her out of the door with me.

"I don't have any breakfast for you, Patches, so you'll have to catch your own," she gave me a look. The name seemed to fit her. She turned away and sauntered off into the long grass.

I looked around. Once I was certain there was no one around, I shifted. The world was instantly clearer in my lynx form. Sounds were sharper and smells stretched out in front of me. I set off for the hills. A couple of deer started when they sensed me. I kept my course, but they still sprinted away. The sheep were more unsettled. I heard bleating and could feel their nervousness. I veered away from them. I raced over the countryside, feeling a freedom I hadn't felt in years. I had had to be so cautious in the city. Here, I could run. I paused at the crest of a hill and sat on my haunches.

Dim lights showed the small towns dotted around. The moon hung low in the sky. A milky crescent. I wouldn't have to worry about the full moon for a little while. My ears swivelled on my head as they picked up trace sounds. A fox scurrying along. The birds starting to wake in their dawn chorus. More lights began to come on in the dwellings around the hill. Time for me to head back. I thrilled in how fast I could go, and even made a game of leaping from rock to rock on the way back. I had forgotten how wild it was up here. In the distance, an engine started up.

I skirted back onto the footpath around the fields, back into the more managed farmland. I kept low and to the edge of the field, my tawny colouring blending well with the dry crops in the fields. I smelled cigarette smoke. Not close. I sped up. My paws pounding the soft ground. With a leap, I cleared the boundary into my own property. I stretched in the shadow of the barn. That felt good.

A noisy engine caused my ears to twitch. An early morning driver on the road. My eyes narrowed as I heard it turn onto my own dirt road. The crunch of gravel and twang of the grass stems being squashed told me they were close.

I lay down in the long grass and watched. A whiff of foul cigarette smoke hit my nostrils. It was the same van from the garage. My body automatically tensed and I forced myself to still.

One of them got out of the van. He was holding a gun. He sighted along it. "Dammit! I can't see anything here. You sure you saw a lion?"

Dzrak, I cursed inwardly in Dwarfish. I had been seen.

"You saw it too!"

"Hey isn't this the Jones place?" The blonde one lowered his gun, "Want to have some fun?"

His buddy grinned, tugging his baseball cap down on his head. They walked towards the main house. I weighed my options up. I had no doubt I was better trained in combat than they were, but it would only take a stray bullet to seriously mess up my day. It would take time to heal and there were two of them. I heard them try the door. It was locked. They circled round. I heard them climb in through the broken kitchen window.

"Hey little lady, you here?"

That settled it. I shifted back to my human form. Hugging the walls, I let myself into the guest house. I grabbed my crossbow from the side, where I'd left it and tucked a knife into my waistband. I dialled 999 on my phone, crouching in the one corner of the room where I had signal and called it in. Armed burglary in progress. The operator seemed surprised when I gave exact co-ordinates. Guess they didn't get a lot of trouble round here. I arched my back to look out of the small window. When I glanced back at the phone, the line had gone dead. I had lost signal.

Cursing softly, I picked up my handbag with the spare crossbow bolts in it and scurried over to their van. It was unlocked. I twisted the keys out of the ignition. They wouldn't get away before the police got here. Then I sprinted back over to the barn. More cover there. I crouched behind something large covered by an old musty tarpaulin.

They had realised I wasn't in the house and were coming back around when I called out to them from the barn. "You're trespassing! I have called the police!"

The blonde one clocked that I was pointing some sort of weapon at them. I watched him squint as he couldn't quite make out what it was in the gloom of the barn. He nodded to his friend and held his gun upright. A gesture of peace. His friend followed suit.

"It's alright sugar, we were just trying to find a lion we saw. You haven't seen anything have you?" He gave what he thought was a subtle jerk of his head to his friend. Baseball cap started to move around in a shoddy pincer movement.

"Not a good idea!" I fired a warning shot. The bolt whistled through the air and landed between his feet. Baseball cap pissed himself. Literally. I saw his pale cargo shorts darken and the breeze carried the acid tang of urine to my nose.

"What the hell?!"

I reloaded fast while their attention was on the bolt.

"Now, now, we've just come here all friendly like. Looks like you've got a lot of work needs doing in the house. Just so happens we're builders. I'll give you a discount…"

"I wouldn't employ you to flush my toilet!"

He was angry now. I saw his fists clench. But he wasn't quite stupid enough to aim his gun. Not yet anyway. "You stupid bitch! You wouldn't be so cocky without a weapon!"

"And you won't be either if you don't turn around and leave, or I'll take your weapon with my next shot." I lowered my crossbow pointedly. It was now aiming at his crotch.

He glowered at me. He was too prideful to back down. I considered my options. Actually hitting them with a bolt would cause me a lot of trouble. I didn't want the paperwork. Going out in the open meant they could shoot me. I was trapped in my own barn. My blood boiled. We were at an impasse.

My keen hearing picked up the welcome sound of sirens approaching. I was annoyed I'd had to call for help but I allowed myself a smile. Impasse over. Their heads turned as they heard the wailing sirens too.

The blonde's icy blue eyes found mine. "You haven't seen the last of us," he ground out. To his credit, he lowered his weapon and didn't run.

A screech of gravel and then two police officers arrived in blue uniforms. They took in the scene and raised their own handguns. Baseball cap immediately dropped his weapon and raised his hands.

"In trouble again Biggels? Let's get down the station."

A rustle of grass made us all turn our heads. Biggels raised his gun at the grass. Collectively we held our breath. My cat friend pushed through, carrying something half her size through the long grass. She gave him one look and ran off.

"There's your lion!" I called.

Relieved laughter filled the air and the police officer patted Biggels on the back, "Still chasing that rumour huh? Come on, let's go."

Reluctantly and with a face like thunder, Biggels handed over his own weapon. Both men were bundled into the back of the car. The female police officer took my statement down. She was clearly angling for me to be a damsel in distress but I was more annoyed that I hadn't been able to handle two mundane humans by myself. She raised her eyebrows at my crossbow but, once I'd shown her my own Magical Liaison Office badge, she was satisfied.

I watched them drive off, dust clouds filling the air. With a smug smile, I headed back to the guest house. I found the cat on the iron steps leading to the front door, with a fresh bird dead between her paws. She looked up as I approached. I stepped over her as she flattened her ears back. As if I'd try to fight her over a wood pigeon.

"Nice catch Patches," I acknowledged, tickling her behind one ear to thank her for her part in confusing the two idiots earlier, "but you're eating that outside."

Chapter 7

I poured myself a black coffee with shaking hands, grateful I had splashed out on the quality beans at the supermarket. I still had adrenaline to burn after the encounter with Tweedle Dumb and Tweedle Dumber.

I stepped into the warm summer air and surveyed the land. My eyes came to rest back on the barn. I walked over to it and impulsively pulled the old tarpaulin off the odd shape. My old quadbike! I ran my fingers over its rims. My thoughts turned to good times as a teenager racing around the fields and roads on this thing. I considered taking it out for a spin. I made it as far as retrieving the remaining can of diesel before I stopped myself. It would be fun, sure. But I wanted to make progress on this place. With a longing look and a promise to myself to ride it later, I filled up the ride on mower instead.

After some frantic pulling at the old-fashioned choke start and a couple of well-placed kicks, the motor chugged into life. More diesel fumes filled the air. I pulled my t-shirt up like a face mask and climbed on.

The cold, metal seat was as uncomfortable as I remembered. I coaxed the machine forward. I nearly lost my balance. I'd forgotten how jerky this thing was. Out of the enclosed barn, I dropped my makeshift facemask back down. I engaged the blades and headed straight for the nearest patch of long grass. It cut through it easily. I allowed myself a fist pump of joy. I revved the small engine and carried on. Small insects left the ground in droves as I ploughed through the grass. It wasn't quick but it was oh so satisfying. I cut through the grass in rows, leaving piles of stalks in my wake. It was only when the sun was high above me and I ran out of fuel that I stopped. I patted the mower affectionately and left it where it had conked out. I headed inside for a drink and something to eat.

"Still here huh, Patches?" The small cat opened one lazy eye and then curled up again on the sofa. I shook my head and rooted around in the cupboards for my remaining food. I settled for a pack of limp croissants and an apple. I set it all on a plate and took it outside to find a patch of shade. I leant against a gnarled tree and took a large bite of apple.

My phone rang. I checked the screen, surprised to get signal. An unknown number flashed up. I frowned at it and picked up.

"Hello," it was meant to sound assertive but the apple in my mouth muffled my greeting.

"Uh hello, is that Ms Jones?"

"Speaking," I was unused to being called anything other than Agent Jones and I was wary. I didn't recognise the deep voice on the line and, was that a twang of an American accent?

"Uh, hi, I'm Dick Anderson. I saw your ad online…for the cottage. Is it still available?"

I sat up straighter, "Yes, yes of course. Are you interested?"

"Uh yes. Definitely. Actually…I was wondering if I could come over tomorrow?" I was silent. Dick waited a beat before continuing, "Your ad did say it was available immediately…"

"Are you in some sort of trouble?"

"No, not at all!"

I cursed inwardly at my suspicious nature. He was just a nice normal person who wanted a holiday rental. I brightened my voice, "Yes, yes it is. Tomorrow would be perfect. What sort of time?"

"I'll need to check the maps, say after lunch?"

"Sounds great. I'll text you the coordinates."

"Uh, how about a post code?"

"Sure, that's what I meant. See you tomorrow." I hung up. That had been quicker than I expected. Who knew there was so much demand for rural cottages? I tried to search his name online. I was still a suspicious person after all, but the flashing bars in the top right corner of my phone screen told me I wasn't getting any internet. I sighed and pocketed the phone. I finished my lunch in a positive mood before it hit me. I had to get the cottage ready for someone to stay in and find somewhere I could sleep. I swore. I hadn't planned this through. I stared at the patch of grass I had managed to clear. It suddenly looked insignificant compared to the scale of the work I had to do. I stared at it as if that could somehow magically make the small field look less messy. I squared my shoulders as if I was preparing to do battle. I would get this place in order. Starting with the small outbuilding where this Dick Anderson would be staying.

I shooed Patches outside and cleaned everything again. I aired musty blankets and sheets outside and threw all the windows open. It still had a dusty smell to me. With a sigh, I headed into town. Claire rushed out of the bakery as I arrived.

"It was great to see you last night!"

"Yeah, you too."

"How's it going at the house?"

"Good, good. Actually, thanks for your idea - someone's going to rent the small cottage."

"Wow! That's great! When are they coming?"

"Tomorrow…I'm trying to get ready."

"Ahhh lovely, are you getting them a nice bottle of wine as a welcome gift?"

That hadn't even occurred to me, "Sure, sure. I also need to grab a sleeping bag so I can rough it in the main house."

Claire offered me her spare room but I turned her down. I wanted to stay on site. It would be easier to do work on the place if I was living there and Vass could find me when he finally remembered to send me something to look at. It wasn't as if I could log into the Magical Liaison Office database with no internet. Claire looked as if she wanted to argue but instead thought for a moment.

Claire came through, "Try Ivor's, they do camping stuff. Might have a sleeping bag. I'd better get back to the shop." She turned as a small child yelled out of the doorway.

"Mummy I need a poo!" Claire shrugged at me and with a final wave headed back inside, ushering her blonde son ahead of her.

"See you," I stuffed my hands in my pockets and headed over to Ivor's hardware store. The paint was peeling off the ancient green sign and it looked closed. I tried the handle anyway and was surprised when it opened. My eyes took a second to adjust to the gloomy interior. It wasn't that there wasn't any light getting it. There were two huge windows at the front and a bare bulb hung from the ceiling. There was just stuff everywhere. Pans were stacked up haphazardly next to garden tools on utilitarian shelving units. I stared. How was I going to find anything? The scent of dust, plastic and oil assaulted me. I curled my lip as I made my way further into the shop, staring around me.

"Welcome to the cave of wonders, are you looking for something in particular?"

The voice startled me and I turned to meet the eyes of a small man with greying hair and thick glasses. I was about to tell him I was just browsing, my stock response in shops, but it wasn't like I'd be able to find anything in here without his help.

"Yes, I'm after camping equipment. Gas stove, sleeping bags. That type of thing. Please."

"Right this way," he led the way to the very back of the store with a shuffling step. I followed as he picked his way around several large and if I'm honest, hideous plastic frogs in various poses. I ducked under a hosepipe swinging from a hook. He stopped abruptly and gestured at a shelf near the back door. I caught myself before I walked into his back.

"Here you go, help yourself. There's sleeping bags in the bedding section." I followed the direction of his finger to a pile of pillows and duvets stacked up against a wall.

He disappeared as I turned back to the camping equipment. "Thank you," I called into the empty shop. I rubbed the back of my neck as I thought about what I'd need. I picked up a camping stove, a small plug in fridge and a camp-bed. I left my selection on the floor and picked out a sleeping bag and a pillow from the pile of bedding. I checked it wasn't stuffed with feathers. That would really mess up my sleep if my inner lynx thought it was surrounded by birds. Luckily there was a foam option. I created a pile of my own and lifted it easily. Carrying it back to the till was another matter. I went slowly. I managed to kick over a gnome and knock over a pile of colanders on my way through. The sound of metal hitting the concrete floor reverberated around the shop.

"Deary me," Ivor's voice sounded from near the front.

"I'll pick it up." I was annoyed and my voice was more growly than I wanted. I deposited my items on the crowded countertop and waded back over to the colanders. I set them upright and shoved them back on the shelf. I looked around for the gnome. It was on its side, trousers down and pretending to pee into a fake wishing well. The figure was missing his nose. Great. Looked like I was buying that too. I picked the offensive garden ornament and slammed the gnome and his nose onto the counter.

"You'll want some superglue for that too," the item was added to my shopping before I could protest. "Anything else?"

In truth I was annoyed and wanted nothing more than to be out of the shop but I forced myself to think. I needed spare gas for the small camping stove and bulbs for the main house. I had no idea whether the fixings were screw or bayonet bulb settings so I bought a couple of each. As a back-up, I grabbed an electric camping lantern too. That would do. The shopkeeper named his price and I handed over my card.

"Need a hand?" he asked helpfully as I began to pile everything up.

"I got this, thanks though," he watched me edge my way to the door. From this side it was pull rather than push. I tried to use my elbow to hook it open.

"Shall I get that for you?"

His offer of help made me more determined to do it myself. My pile wobbled dangerously but I managed to open the door. Using my leg to hold it open, I stepped through. I crammed everything into the boot of my sedan car and slammed the lid shut. I pinched the bridge of my nose as I tried to think. My stomach rumbled. Food.

At the supermarket, I selected items I thought would last and bought a tin opener. It was lower quality than the hardware store but I didn't fancy going back in there today. I also grabbed a lavender scented candle and some fabric freshener. The place might not look like much but it was going to smell great. As I walked past the small alcohol aisle, I remembered Claire's comment. A welcome bottle of wine. I selected one red, one white and one for me. What else made people feel welcome? A cheap bunch of flowers caught my eye. Perfect. The lady behind the counter again upsold me a canvas bag. I had to start to remember to bring carrier bags with me or I was going to lose a small fortune.

With my food stashed on the backseat and the flowers on the passenger seat so they didn't get squashed, I pulled out. I needed more diesel for the mower. One more stop before I start the drive back home. I tapped my finger on the steering wheel. Home. I hadn't thought that place was home in a long time. Weird. I almost missed the turning for the garage as I contemplated that. Pull yourself together Jones, I chided myself as I executed a sharp turn. The flowers slid off the seat and into the foot well. I swore.

Back at the small cottage, I left the wine on the side. There was no vase for the flowers so I took a set of cutlery and a plate and mug back to the main house with me and went hunting. I didn't find a vase but did find an old cream jug. It looked quaint in an old farm sort of way. I put the flowers in it and tried to arrange them nicely. I gave up. How were they already wilting? Annoyed, I looked around the outbuilding. It was clean. I set the scented candle next to the flowers. The lavender scent was strong to my sensitive nose. I sprayed everything else with the fabric freshener and a clean lemony scent filled the air. I sniffed appreciatively. Reluctantly I left the cosy cottage back for the main house. Mould and damp and dust assaulted me. I forced myself forwards and opened the windows downstairs. I had limited options on where I was going to stay. My old room had a tree growing in it. No way was I going in Mum's room. Too many memories. The kitchen window was broken. That left the lounge.

I set up the camp bed next to the sofa. One metal leg got stuck. I cursed as I forced it into position. I looked around. My home for however long this Dick wanted to stay here. It was dusty and I spotted a fern growing in one corner. Great. I thought longingly of the small cottage. I could stay there tonight and change the bed tomorrow. Genius. I checked the time on my phone. The sun was setting but I could get a couple of hours of cleaning done in here and then it wouldn't be so bad tomorrow. Pleased at my plan I retrieved my cleaning equipment and covered my sleek hair with a tea towel. Time to get to work. I had taken three steps into the house when a hum caught my ears. I turned and edged forward back towards the door. Not a hum. Wings beating. Large wings. Getting closer.

My hand clenched the feather duster in my hand. My crossbow was back in my handbag. I swore under my breath. I put the rest of the cleaning products down and held the duster in a combat pose. The handle was solid wood and I was trained to use staffs. Dust rose up from the overgrown gravelled drive as a figure landed on top of the builders' abandoned van. It furled its grey wings and surveyed my home. As it turned, I clocked the brown package in its hands before looking at its face.

With a smile, I stepped out of the shadow of the hallway onto the front step.

"Gwendoline!"

“What a dump!” the harpy jumped down and held out one hand. I gripped her forearm in salute. She was in her half human form: all normal except for the giant grey wings and claws on her hands. I was glad she’d chosen that instead of her full harpy form. A giant bird with a human head was pretty freaky to look at. Plus my lynx instinct was to chase it. I could keep that at bay better when she was in this form.

“What are you doing here?”

“Vass told me you needed this,” she thrust the package into my hands, then noticed the duster, “were you going to tickle me to death?! You’re better than that Jones!”

I shrugged as I repositioned the duster and the parcel, “I left my crossbow in my handbag.”

Gwendoline cocked her head to one side, taking in the tea towel tied over my hair like a washerwoman, “You doing OK? Vass said you were on some sort of sabbatical but you’re keeping your hand in with some paperwork?”

“I’m fine, just needed a break you know?”

The harpy shook her head. She didn’t know. She lived for her work. Like me. Except I needed to figure out what was going on at the Office and I could do that better out here. Fewer people to endanger for one.

“OK, well I’ll be off then. Tell Vass I’m not a damn courier service!”

I stepped back and gave her room to take off. She crouched down then leapt into the air, using the thrust to help get her airborne. I watched as her dove-grey wings beat powerfully. In barely a couple of minutes, she was a dot in the horizon, even with my keen senses. I looked at the package now in my hands. A plain packing envelope with my name on it. I sat on the stone step in front of the house. In a practiced motion, I inserted one finger under the tab and made a clean rip along one end. I tipped the file out into my hand. A sticky Post-It note had Vass's handwriting neatly printed on it.

Have fun! V

I narrowed my eyes. Either he'd found something or he was using this as an opportunity to get me to do some grunt work. I opened the manila file and stared at rows of data. Grunt work. Great. There was a red envelope tucked into the folder addressed to me in a scrawl. I tore that open and took out the card. It had a tool box with a large saw sticking out of it printed on the front and the words *I'm saw-ry* in large letters. My lips curled upwards in a smile. Just the sort of stupid pun I appreciated. I opened the card. Maxi's handwriting was hard to read at the best of times. Here it was almost illegible.

Ruth, Sorry I've been a total tool. I am trying to make it up to you here. I know it will take a while to earn your trust again but I won't let you down. I think I found something. Vass says you'll enjoy the tech reports. I'll be in touch soon. Take care of yourself, Maxi.

PS Van now fireproof.

It sounded a bit like a letter he'd write home from the posh school he'd been to but I appreciated the sentiment. It was just a shame I couldn't be a hundred per cent sure this wasn't part of some ruse. I pinched the bridge of my nose. I hated not being able to trust my own team.

As if my thoughts had summoned them, my phone lit up with one of my team's number. I pulled my thoughts back to reality and answered, noting the two bars of signal dropped to one as I lifted my phone from my pocket to my ear.

Chapter 8

"What's going on?"

"Are you here?" Aloora's voice sounded concerned through the phone.

"You know I'm not. I'm still on…leave," I ground the word out between gritted teeth.

"Who's authorised this then?"

"Who's authorised what?" I fought to keep my voice calm against my rising annoyance with the newest team member.

"There are tanks outside the dragon's nest."

I let loose a stream of Dwarfish curse words. "Try to stop them doing anything stupid. I'll make some calls." I hung up and immediately began dialling my contacts. I wished I was there to help but I could do the next best thing.

I started with the armed forces. No one was happy being called in the evening but I wasn't letting this go. Eventually

I confirmed that there was indeed an attack being launched on the dragons' new nesting site in the Millennium Stadium. Great. I worked my way higher up the food chain, pulling rank as far as I could. It was clear no one was backing down. Something about civilian endangerment. I tried to explain that the risk of casualties was higher if the dragons were attacked, but the gruff general I got up to summed it up succinctly, "These creatures can't live alongside people in cities. We have to take them out or move them along. Now I have a dinner to get back to."

That was it then. With another few curses at the phone after he'd hung up, I thought. Where could the dragons live safely? A place whispered through my head. Breconia. The elven reserve had plenty of space, magical wards and was already home to several of the more dangerous magical creatures. I called my contact in the Elven High Council.

"Sylvana, it's Jones here."

"Jones! How are you? Got into trouble with any more manticores lately?"

I smiled at her reference to our previous mission together to contain a manticore that had escaped the confines of Breconia and was terrorising the locals. "Not lately. It's been too long!"

She laughed, then switched to business mode, "I assume this isn't a social call?"

"No, sorry. Dragon problems."

"I heard."

I wasn't surprised. The elves kept themselves involved with all goings on, despite claiming to live apart from the world in their dedicated reserve. "Then you know they're being forced out of Cardiff."

"I would have thought the land of dragons would have been more welcoming to these magnificent creatures."

"Well, there's only so much welcome they can expect when they could destroy the city in less than an hour if they chose to."

"Let me guess, you want them in our nature reserve?"

"Right. You are a safe haven from the modern world…"

"I don't know what you expect me to do about it."

I smiled again, I knew exactly how to play this, "You do owe me after forcing me to take Lorandir onto my taskforce…"

"Come on now Jones, you're better than that!"

"You're right, sorry to bother you. I just thought one of the most progressive members of the Council would relish this chance to aid these ancient magical creatures rather than see them exterminated…"

I heard her intake of breath, "Is it really that bad?"

"Life or death."

"I'll see what I can do, no promises though. The King has to approve any formal applications for sanctuary."

"I'll leave it with you." I was confident this would be our solution. The King would lose a lot of political support in the mundane world if he formally refused a request to house magical beings in need of refuge.

I got a call back almost instantly. “We’ll take them. The King seems very keen to provide a sanctuary for them.”

“Great. How are we going to get them to you?”

“It would be easy if you had any recordings of them making their family calls. We could magically amplify it and draw them here.”

I smiled, “Leave it with me.”

I messaged Dot for her to send me the recordings I knew that the newest member of my team had been making. Aloora sent through the files and I forwarded them on to Sylvana. They sounded loud and angry to my ears, but my dragon expert assured me these weren’t threatening calls.

Satisfied I had done what I could to help the dragons, I texted Dot and Aloora and settled down for the night. I had work to do. I gave up on cleaning and headed back to the cottage for my final night. I poured myself a large glass of wine, pulled a pack of highlighters and a pen from my handbag and began working through the pile of reports in front of me.

I woke with a start. There was a slight pressure on my back. I sat upright and Patches meowed in protest and dug her claws in as she used my back as a launching pad to get to the windowsill. With a flick of her white paws, she disappeared out of the open window. I peeled a piece of paper off of the side of my face. Looks like I’d fallen asleep on top of my work. I looked down. I’d managed to get halfway through the tech and research reports. So far, the spend figures all reconciled to the budget I’d been given. The Magical Liaison Office bureaucracy was a pain but at least everything was written down. All funding requests had been approved, money had been released, money had been spent. Blah blah blah. An analyst with access to the database could have done this job in less than an hour. I'd been up until the small hours of the morning ticking and tying these numbers back. I was sure Vass was enjoying this. I gave up trying to think about which misdemeanour this was a punishment for. I wasn't a model employee but I did things by the book…most of the time. And I got results. It just often seemed to end with him taking a call from the higher ups.

I shoved the paperwork to one side, stretched and made myself a coffee. Maxi had said I'd enjoy the reports, what was I missing? I began to mentally plan my day. A run first to clear my head, then back to the reports. Something niggled at the back of my mind. I got changed and went for a run. I'd figure out what was bothering me later. I stayed in my human form, just in case there were any more lunatics with guns around. The police still hadn't collected the van and it was sitting in my driveway as a stark reminder of yesterday's events. I ignored it and set off on my route. Halfway up a hill, the niggle in my mind jumped forward and I jerked to a stop. The tourist was coming today. Great. My stuff was still in the cottage. The main house was still unfit to live in. The damn reports had distracted me. I had work to do. I turned round and ran back.

As I leapt over a small stream, another thought pinged to the front of my brain. I pulled myself to a stop, trying to think. I had seen Vass' name alongside the Director's on some of those projects. I sprinted back to the house and double checked the signatories against the projects. Vass was on a couple of them. Coincidence? I didn't know any more. I considered calling Maxi but stopped myself. I didn't want to set any wolves running yet.

After a quick shower, I moved all my stuff into the main house. My enchanted handbag made that a quick trip and I sent a silent thank you to the wizard who had crafted it. Then I changed the bed and surveyed the cottage. Still clean. The flowers looked like they were perking up. Good. I took my coffee mug with me and started on the main house. Three hours later and the room I was planning to stay in was clean at least. There was still a mouldy smell but I had dug up the fern growing in one corner and sprayed everything with disinfectant. I had even taken out some of my pent up frustrations on the sofa cushions by taking them outside and pounding the years of dust out of them. It had made me sneeze but was worth it.

The sun was high overhead now. Beads of sweat glistened on my coppery skin. My workout clothes were soaked and sticking to me uncomfortably. I'd made a lot of headway but was still frustrated at how much there was to do. I ran my fingers through my hair. Cobwebs and dust had permeated it, even with the tea towel I had tied over it. I needed another shower. Wistfully, I looked at the small cottage with its working power shower. I refused myself that luxury. I had to at least try out the bathroom in the main house. With trepidation, I walked upstairs and turned the taps on. After a clunk the water began to flow. So far, so good. I reached behind the shower curtain and turned it on. The dial came off in my hand. Dzrak it. Water began to gush from the shower head and a break in the pipe. A spray of water caught me in the face. I wiped my eyes and glared at the hole as if my gaze could seal the leak. I didn't even bother trying to stop it with my hands. Instead I headed back downstairs and turned off all the water to the house. Great. Just what I needed. I pinched the bridge of my nose as I thought. I'd need a trip into town for supplies to fix the pipe. Or I could call Sam. But first I really, really wanted a damn shower. The cottage caught my eye. I could have a quick shower, get changed then go into town…I didn't really have another option. It would be rude to greet my guest in this state. My mind was still working on excuses but my feet decided for me. I was already crossing the short distance to the cottage.

The shower was good. Hot water hit my back and washed away the sweat. I hummed a cheesy pop song to myself as I scrubbed the dirt of the morning away. I got out and wrapped a towel around myself, before selecting a smaller one for my hair. I checked. There was still a spare for the holiday maker coming later. With a smile on my face, I headed outside. I'd left my clothes in my handbag, back at the main house so needed to cross the unkempt driveway to get them. I enjoyed the feel of the grass under my naked feet as I picked my way back to the farmhouse. The sun was overhead and there wasn't a cloud in the sky. I had just got to the chorus of a Spice Girls' classic when my ears picked up the unmistakable roar of a motorbike engine. I paused a few steps from the front door. The bike turned off the main road. Onto my driveway. A dust trail followed it as it headed for me.

I tensed. The driver's head was completely covered by a black helmet. Black motorbike leathers covered his body. I caught him looking at the van still parked in my drive before he came to a stop next to it. I sniffed cautiously. The scent was male and leather mixed with paper. My inner lynx perked up. Those were some attractive smells. I pushed that thought away and moved my legs into a martial arts stance. For all I knew, this was an assassin sent from my own organisation.

Chapter 9

The biker took of his helmet and shook his head, running his fingers through short brown hair. He walked forward and held out his hand to me.

"Pleased to meet you. I'm Dick."

Dzrak. I rearranged the grip on my towel and shook the proffered hand. I noticed his eyebrows raise.

"I'm Jones, Ruth Jones."

"That's one helluva grip you've got there, chief."

I stared at him blankly. What was I meant to say to that?

He tapped his chiselled chin and looked me dead in the eye, as if he was consciously making an effort not to look me up and down. "Am I interrupting something? I'm sorry I wasn't more precise with the times but I wasn't sure how long it would take to get here…"

I wasn't the sort to blush so I narrowed my eyes at him instead. "I was just getting showered. Give me a minute and I'll get dressed and show you to your accommodation." I turned on my heel and stomped into the house. Well that really helped cement a landlady / holiday renter relationship. I pulled on a fitted blouse and tailored trousers, then for good measure added a pair of don't mess with me heels. They didn't suit my surroundings at all but it was my go to armour for work and I needed a confidence boost after getting caught with my clothes off. Literally.

Dick had undone his leather jacket and was now carrying a khaki green carry-all he'd retrieved from a pannier.

"This way please," I was all business. I strode over to the cottage and he followed at an easier pace in my wake. He was still a few steps behind me as I powered up the iron steps and into the small dwelling. I folded my arms as he entered the place and took a look around. I waited for him to take it all in.

He gave a low whistle, "Nice place ya got here, real nice. Reminds me of a novel. Perfect."

I chose to ignore that, "Well here's the cottage…this is the kitchen, obviously, the bedroom's back there and there's a bathroom behind that door." I noticed Patches curled up on the sofa. I tried to discreetly shoo her out. She stared at me as only cats can stare and stayed where she was.

He stepped inside and looked around, depositing his carry-all on the small sofa next to the cat. He gave her a little scratch under the chin and was rewarded with a thunderous purr from deep within her chest. If he was surprised that there was a pet in his new home, he was gracious enough not to mention it. He picked up a bottle of wine and studied the label with an approving nod. “And will we be sharing a shower?” His brown eyes met mine with a crinkle of amusement.

I narrowed my own eyes, “What do you mean?”

“You were using this bathroom earlier right? I just meant do we need to set up a schedule or something?”

“No.” Aware I was being rude and I needed him to stay, I expanded, “I mean, I’ve got a temporary issue with the shower in the main house. I’m fixing it today. In fact I’d better go get some supplies.” I turned and hurried down the steps.

“Hey, I didn’t mean to upset you or nothing, maybe I could join you if you’re going into town? Gotta get my bearings if I’m going to be here a while.”

I paused and turned back, “How long are you planning to stay for Mr Anderson?”

“It’s Dick and how does three months sound to start with? Would that be alright, chief?”

“Yes, perfect. I’ll need a month in advance for a deposit.”

“Sure thing,” he whipped out his phone to make a transfer then moved it around in the universal martial art poses for needing a signal.

I smiled and decided to be friendly, “Signal’s a bit patchy round here. Try the bedroom or the barn.”

“How about town? That’s gotta have signal right? You can give me the tour.” He smiled revealing a set of dazzling white teeth. Dammit. I guessed he was making sense. I could at least give him directions to town. I started to explain the route when he interrupted me, "I can follow you on the bike."

I nodded and grabbed my handbag before climbing into my dull, dust-covered Volvo. I didn't wait to check he was following me as I drove off towards the town. I parked up and heard the motorbike rumble to a stop behind me. No chance of avoiding my new house guest then. I ran my fingers through my hair unconsciously to neaten it before stepping out on to the road.

"I've got to get a few things," I turned on my high heels and headed for Ivor's hardware store. This time I went straight in. I strode to where I thought I remembered seeing some pipes and glared at the metal tubes leaning against a shelving unit.

"Can I help you there?" the shopkeeper's familiar voice sounded through the dim shop.

"I've got a leak in the shower." Behind me, I heard the door open and close again. Then a low whistle.

"This is some kinda place." Dammit, Dick had followed me in.

Ivor waved at the newcomer and then selected a pipe and a role of plumber's tape for me. He stared at me hard as I paid, before his eyes lit up in recognition.

"Back again is it? I thought I recognised your voice. You doing plumbing dressed like that?"

"I expect I'll change first," I bit out the words, not enjoying being the butt of anyone's joke.

Dick moved closer to the counter, still looking round at the hardware. “Plastic frogs huh?”

“Some say they’re lucky, you know. I think this one is my favourite,” Ivor stepped out from behind the counter to grab a frog wearing a crown and puckering its green lips.

“Lucky frogs?”

I grabbed my things and made for the door. In my haste, I nearly bumped into Sam coming in.

“Sorry Miss.”

“No trouble…actually, thank you for the quote. I wanted to ask when you’re free to start work.”

He looked at me for a minute before he did a double take. I was slightly offended at all these double takes. I did not look that different in my smarter clothes. He took in the length of pipe in my hand.

“Looks like you’re starting without me!”

“Plumbing issue.”

“Tell you what, I’ll pop by tomorrow and check it out if you like?”

“Thanks, that’s really kind.”

He shrugged, “Least I can do. We can finalise the specs for the job then too. I know you wanted to do a lot yourself.”

I smiled, glad that he had really listened to me the other day. Dick appeared at my shoulder.

“Where’s next then tour guide?”

I rolled my eyes.

Sam stifled a laugh, "Well, see you tomorrow. Nice to meet you." He stood back to let us pass and I led the way back onto the high street. As I turned to ask Dick where he wanted to go, I noticed with horror that the plastic frog was carefully tucked under one arm.

"I can't believe you actually bought that monstrosity!"

"I think it's kinda cute."

"I think I might have to instigate a no garden ornament policy on my holiday rental."

He laughed, a rich throaty sound that had me smiling in response. I quickly regained my composure. I was here to work not laugh with attractive strangers.

"Right, so where do you want to go now?"

He contemplated, then shrugged, "How about finding some food?"

"I can recommend the bakery, my friend works there, and the supermarket is alright. I haven't been in the local pub since I was a teenager so no idea if it's any good."

He nodded, a tinge of amusement creasing his eyes, "Let's check out this bakery."

I darted across the road and into Claire's shop. His long legs easily kept up with my brisk pace. Claire smiled as we entered. There was a gleam in her eye. I guessed she'd seen us walking along the road.

"You didn't tell me you were bringing a handsome man out here Ruth!"

“He’s renting out the cottage Claire. You know, like you suggested the other day.”

“I see, well hello there mister.”

“Hi there, Dick Anderson, pleasure to meet you miss.”

I watched my friend blush as she shook his hand then packaged up a baguette and six Welsh cakes, filled with plump raisins.

“You know, you look very familiar…are you on TV?”

“Claire!”

“No, no not on TV,” he actually looked a little uncomfortable. Interesting.

“You’ll both have to come over, I know Sam’s been dying to see you. I’ll message you,” Claire waved us out of her shop.

“Now, what can we get to go with this bread?”

“Supermarket’s that way,” I gestured over the road to the small shop.

“Great, I want to hear all about the local delicacies.”

After he’d bought up pretty much everything that had ‘made in Wales’ stamped on in, and been sold one of the canvas bags - surely the supermarket was running low on them - we walked the rest of the high street. I slowed my pace so he could take it all in. Dick looked around with interest, admiring the quaint houses.

“Still here are you?”

I looked round to see who was shouting and sighed when I saw it was the two idiots who had been at the farm yesterday. They had clearly been released already. Thank you British justice system. I rose to their bait without thinking. "There's no law about me walking down the street!"

"There should be!"

"We'll be out to get our van back, just wait."

That didn't sound good, "Set one foot on my property and I'll call the police." I deliberately spoke loudly so the few people about could hear me. It was important that I did things by the book here.

One of them gave me a rude gesture. It went well with his *'sup ladies'* t-shirt. Really classy.

"What was that about?" Dick was curious. Great. The last thing I needed was a curious house guest.

"Just some trouble with the locals."

I shook my head and turned away. I heard the slur that they called after me. I clenched my fists, feeling my rage boil up and my inner lynx strain to be released. I knew I could take them out easily, but the echoes of Mum held me back. *Education, not violence Ruth. Violence is not going to solve our problems.* Violence wasn't always the answer, but it felt good. I forced myself to breathe calmly and unclench my fists. They weren't worth it. I had bigger problems to deal with. Like a Director who had raised a damned dragon. Dick wasn't so tolerant.

"Where I come from that's not a nice word," he took a step towards the two men.

“What are you going to do about it, leathers? Think you’re hard?” The leader moved two paces towards us.

Tensions were rising fast. Dick handed me his frog and put his canvas bag on the pavement. He cracked his knuckles and took another step forward. His large frame towered over the two men. I smelled the fear pouring off the cowards. Fear mixed with adrenaline. Idly, I wondered if any of them actually knew how to fight. The shouting had drawn a small crowd of locals, watching with undisguised interest. I pinched the bridge of my nose and stepped forward myself. This was bloody ridiculous. I didn’t need anyone to fight my battles for me. Shoving the frog into Dick’s chest, I took control of the situation.

“Enough! They’re not worth it!” I noted the surprise in his eyes as my shove forced him to take a step backwards. I turned to my bully, “And you, do you kiss your mother with that mouth? Back off and leave me alone or I’ll report you for harassment.”

Was that relief flashing over his rat-like face? He didn’t take the opportunity to back down though. Idiot. “Get a girl to fight for you will you?” He ignored me and shouted over my shoulder at Dick.

That was when I lost my cool. I stepped forward. Grabbing his arm, I twisted it cruelly behind his back. He shouted in pain as I used my height and supernatural strength to lever his arm up, forcing him to his knees. His friend took a step towards me and I snarled a warning at him. I knew my amber eyes were flashing with anger. His body had a survival instinct even if he didn’t. He wasn’t top of the food chain here. He took a step backwards and held up his hands in an appeasing gesture. Satisfied I wasn’t going to get any trouble from that direction, I turned my attention back to the snivelling man on the ground in front of me.

"This woman doesn't need anyone to fight for her, right?"

He nodded furiously.

"You are a stupid bigot who needs to brush up on his vocabulary."

More nodding.

"You will leave me and my friends alone, do you understand?"

He nodded. I squeezed his arm. "Arg, yes, yes!"

"I'm going to let go now. You are going to get up and walk away. Yes?"

"Y…Yes!"

I released his arm. He came up swinging his good hand towards my face. I had expected him to do something stupid. I stepped nimbly to one side and stuck out my foot, using his own momentum to trip him up. He landed face first on the hard uneven pavement. His arm connected second and he cried out in pain. I walked away and joined Dick who had an amazed look on his face.

"You sure can handle yourself huh?"

I nodded, "I can…so don't get on my bad side."

He laughed and looked back where the would-be assailant was nursing a nose bleed. "Oh I don't intend to!"

I gave a small snort of laughter and we crossed the road. A uniformed special constable in a high vis jacket had wandered over to the small crowd and asked what happened. My keen ears picked up the general consensus was that Billy had tripped. I felt my grin spreading. Violence wasn't the answer but sometimes it felt good to put bigots in their place.

Back at our vehicles, I watched Dick struggle to get the large frog into his bike pannier with a wry smile on my face.

"I don't suppose it would be too much trouble for me to ask you to take her back in the car?"

"You want me to take that…thing back in my car?" I responded with mock horror.

"It's a big favour to ask…" he met my eyes with his chocolate brown ones, "…how bout I make you dinner tonight in exchange for you lookin' after Philippa here?"

"You named it?!" He shrugged and held the hideous ornament out to me. I opened the boot and gestured.

"I can't believe you're not letting her ride up front!"

"You're lucky I'm giving her any space in there. If you push it, I'll make sure the ride back is nice and bouncy for her. For it!"

"You drive a hard bargain!"

I shut the lid hard, plunging the plastic frog into darkness.

Chapter 10

Back at the house, Dick rescued the frog ornament from my car and I lugged the length of pipe into the bathroom. Then I started searching for tools. I wasn't going to wait for Sam to fix my bathroom if I could do it. I found a set of screwdrivers under the kitchen sink. The jackdaw dive bombed me as I entered the room.

"You are going to be the first thing to go in this house!" I shouted after the bird as it flew out of the broken window.

Dick must have heard me because he materialised behind me soon after, "Did you call?"

"Just shouting at a jackdaw."

He shrugged like that was a normal answer and I didn't sound like a crazy lady, "Whatcha doin'?"

"Looking for some tools, I wanted to get started on the pipework so I can turn the water back on but all I can find are these," I gestured to the screwdriver set. Dick's eyes took in the pink handles. Mum had been all for girl power and self-reliance in a very feminine way.

"Hmmm…" he rubbed his jaw. The stubble gave him a rugged look in keeping with his creased leather jacket, faded cotton t-shirt and casual jeans. If I'd been the type to notice that sort of thing, I would have said it was an extremely attractive look. "Well there's a van outside, there might be tools in there."

"That's not my van."

"Who's van is it?"

"You met them today."

He frowned as he pieced it together then shrugged, "OK, let's take a look."

"It doesn't feel right," I crossed my arms.

He stared at me in disbelief. "From what I saw today, some racist bastards drove their van onto your property and then harassed you…"

"Aimed a gun at me more like," I mumbled.

"Exactly, they are not the good guys here. I'm sure they could lend you some tools, it'll be good karma for them. We'll put them right back…"

He was making some kind of sense but I still didn't like it. I shook my head reluctantly, "I'll check the barn, maybe there's some wrenches there."

I left Dick standing there while I pounded over to the large barn. It was worse for wear too but was holding up better than the main house. I dug around in boxes, pulling out spare lawnmower parts and old magazines. I really needed to go through all this junk. I patted my old quadbike, promising myself a ride in the near future. I heard Dick's long strides crunching across the gravel towards the barn and looked up. He had a strange sort of smirking grin on his face like he'd just done something bad and was proud of it. He stopped just inside the barn and leaned easily against an upright beam, keeping his hands behind his back.

I raised my eyebrow, "What?"

"This any good?" He moved his arm from behind his body and showed off a large black toolbox. I didn't recognise it.

I pursed my lips, "And where did you find that?"

He shrugged, "Just lyin' around. It's got a wrench in it." He showed me his other hand, which was indeed holding a wrench.

I met his gaze and my lips twitched before I could help myself. He must have seen my slip in self-control because his smile widened.

"Come on, I'll help ya out."

"OK, but then you are putting those straight back where you found them!"

"Yes ma'am," he did a smart salute without hitting his forehead with the wrench. Impressive.

I led the way back to the house and upstairs to the small bathroom. He took in the dust and the décor without comment as he peeled off his jacket and looked at the pipework. He got straight to work while I leaned on the doorframe and watched.

"You a plumber then Dick?"

"Nah, just had to fix my share of DIY issues back home."

"Where's home?"

"Here and there," I fixed him with my amber eyes and he rolled his shoulders before giving me a proper answer, "I was born near Oxford but we moved around a lot and I've spent the past few years stateside. I guess that's what I'd call home, at least…it was…" He trailed off as he stared somewhere into middle distance behind the shower. He shook his head and came back to the present, "And is this your home?"

I looked around the bathroom and nodded, "Yeah, I grew up here. Been gone awhile but I guess it's still home."

"Home is where the heart is, huh?"

It was a question, and I grunted my agreement but inside I was uncomfortable. Was my heart here in rural Wales? Would I have let this place go to ruin if I really loved it? Maybe I should just sell the damn place and be done with it. I scowled at myself for that thought. I couldn't do that to Mum. The piece of my heart that longed to have her back wouldn't let me sell the farm. To distract myself from my thoughts, I watched Dick as he detached the broken pipe and capped off the water source. He looked at ease and he hummed softly while he worked. He noticed me watching him and gave me a wink. I narrowed my eyes at him then remembered he was doing me a favour, not that I'd asked him to. "Shall I make us a cup of tea?"

He snorted a laugh, "That's so British! I'd love one. Milky with two sugars please."

I left the room quickly before I said something I regretted. I walked the short distance to the small cottage and made the drinks in there. I ignored the crowned frog ornament that he'd set prominently on the side as I poured milk into his cup. I preferred mine black. He entered just as I'd finished brewing the teabags. He washed his hands before grabbing a tea towel and drying them. Patches sauntered in and began winding herself around his ankles. She was definitely choosing a favourite. I tried to ignore the ridiculous pang of jealousy I felt towards the small feline as he bent down to give her a stroke before looking up at me.

"Well it's capped off so you can turn your water on again, but the pipe you got needs cuttin' down to size before I can fit it."

I nodded and offered him a mug, "Thanks. I mean I could have done it myself but thank you."

He stood with a look of amusement on his face, "Oh no doubt, chief, and you're welcome."

I looked away and took another drink before remembering that this was his place now. "Right, well you know where I am if you need anything. I'll get out of your hair."

"Stay. I'll make us some food."

I still had a pile of paperwork to look through but food sounded appealing, "Well I guess you do still owe me for transporting that amphibian monstrosity!"

"Hey, Philippa has feelings you know!" he covered either side of the statue's head where ears would have been. I shook my head in mock disgust and leaned back against the small kitchen countertop.

With a smile, Dick began opening cupboards and finding pots and pans. He handed me a knife and a chopping board when I asked if I could help and set me to work on dicing vegetables. The onion stung my nose fiercely and I blinked back tears angrily, annoyed that an allium was causing me to show weakness. Wordlessly, he opened the bottle of red wine I had left out on the side as a welcoming gift. He poured us both large glasses.

"Thanks. It's the onions, they always get me." I didn't want him to think I started crying for no reason. I moved the knife quickly and aggressively to finish cutting the offending onion before placing the chopping board next to him, and retreating to other side of the small kitchen. It was still potent and my eyes only stopped streaming once he had cooked it off. My mouth began to water as he placed thin steaks into the pan.

He moved with ease as he checked on the food. When he plated up the steaks and sauté potatoes, I was impressed.

"So you're a handyman and you can cook, bet you get all the girls."

His face seemed to cloud over for a second before he replied, "Never the right one."

I didn't want to dig into his love life so I changed the subject rapidly, "So what are you planning to do while you're here?"

"I want to get closer to nature, go for walks, get inspired. I just wanted some time to think really, it's too busy in the city."

"Is that where you've been staying?"

"Yeah, London's great but it's too crowded for what I need right now."

We chatted about London for a while, bemoaning the crowded underground tubes and the traffic. We found we shared a mutual love of the green spaces there. My favourite park was Hyde Park. Its large area and tree coverings were perfect for full moon runs. He preferred St James's Park with its picturesque lake. I found myself smiling. I was actually enjoying talking to someone without it being about work. It was a strange sensation. I had to pull myself away.

"Well, this has been nice, but I should go…I've got work to do."

He gave me a look, "You're not goin' to work on the house this late are ya?!"

"No, this is for my real job."

"What do you do?"

"I work for a government department, the Magical Liaison Office."

"Sounds fun."

"If your idea of fun is wading through paperwork and creating reports then sure, I guess it's fun…no it's OK, just a bit disillusioned with it all at the moment."

"I get that. Can I help?"

"How good are you at reconciling numbers?"

"Er…"

"Just kidding. Enjoy the rest of your evening."

"Sure. Hey, you know, I could help out…with the house I mean. I renovated a place over in the States."

"I mean, sure if you want to, but aren't you here on holiday? You could see the sights, go for walks…" I trailed off. I was not a good tour guide.

"I'll do that too, but I'd like to keep busy. You'd be doin' me a favour, honestly."

"Well I guess I can't say no to that! Thanks, I'd really appreciate it, just make sure you tell me if you feel I'm taking advantage."

He shot me a look. It wasn't a look I was used to getting. He almost smouldered, "I'm looking forward to it."

I stood up quickly, "Well, bye." Patches immediately jumped up and settled in my vacated spot.

He gave me a sideways smile from his seat on the sofa as I left the small cottage. What was that about? I was already regretting my decision to rent out the cottage. I didn't need any distractions. Pulling my thoughts away from sexy house guests, I decided to call Dot. The sun had set and the vampire would be at work. I walked around the house until my phone got some signal. She picked up straight away.

"What is it? Is everything alright?"

“Everything’s fine. Vass has got me checking research reports. I think I’m going to end up clearing up all the Office’s admin tasks before I’m done.”

“No leads then?”

“Nothing concrete. Did your contacts in London come up with anything?” The vampire’s social circles were a lot wider than mine, but then she had been alive for a few centuries.

“Only that the Director is very private. Never goes into any vampire clubs, no vices we know of, and you know we know a lot about vices…the only place he seems to go is a private gentlemen’s club. Anything else I can help with?”

“No. Thanks for the offer, but this needs to stop with me. I can’t have any of you put at risk. How’s Aloora settling in after Stonehenge?”

“Fine. She’s taken it surprisingly well. She thinks you should forgive Maxi and take him back onto the team. I think she’s been messaging him.”

I ignored her comment about Maxi, He’d have to prove himself first. I went through the internal management procedures guide in my mind. There wasn’t a section on dragon attacks but there was definitely something about trauma at work. “Have you offered her counselling?”

“Of course! But I actually think she loved seeing the dragons. She’s loving our library and planning about a hundred research projects. She’s asked to stake out the dragons’ nesting site and...I might take her out on some field work one evening.”

I heard the smile in Dot's voice and instantly grew suspicious, "What sort of field work?"

"Maybe take her to some supernatural haunts, start introducing her to some contacts…the quarterly city supernatural board is coming up, maybe she could represent the Office there."

"Nice try! You know I need you there to represent the Office and keep an ear to the ground. She can shadow you if you want company but you're my deputy, I need you there."

The vampire groaned. I knew she hated those meetings, but I wasn't ready to delegate to a complete newbie more interested in books than supernatural politics.

"I'll make it up to you when I get back," I promised.

"Fine, but next time Cirian's playing, I want security detail!"

I chuckled, Dot's love of the elven singer was well-known in the Office, "Deal."

"So how's the house?" the vampire's voice softened.

"You know, a wreck. I'm starting to do it up though, so that'll keep me busy when I'm not doing paperwork."

"A normal person would use an enforced sabbatical to relax," I heard the concern in her voice.

"Well between trying to get evidence of a conspiracy at work, living in a wreck and having a handsome house guest I'm finding it difficult to relax!"

"Handsome house guest? That sounds like it should be easy to relax. Tell me more."

Great. I'd said too much. "Not much to tell. I needed some money to do up the house so I'm renting out the cottage. This guy was interested, said he wants to soak in the scenery or something."

" 'Or something' sounds more interesting…this could be just what you need boss. No, listen," she carried on before I could say anything, "You're always working, I don't think you've had a holiday since you transferred to Cardiff and I certainly don't remember you having any dates…"

I interrupted, "There was that one guy I had coffee with, you know, the warlock who came to the Office that time…"

"Contractors don't count! Especially ones fixing the printer! Now listen to me, I know you're going to work but try to have some fun as well. Go for long walks with the attractive human and try to loosen up. Have fun, enjoy yourself! Take it from someone older and wiser. I'm not saying get laid…but if you want to…" she trailed off. I could almost hear her waggling her eyebrows suggestively.

I knew she was right but I couldn't let her have it all her own way. I let out an exasperated sigh, "If I agree to relax, will you get off my case?"

"Sure, and Jones?"

"Yeah?"

"When you do have sex with him, I want details!" She hung up. I glared at my phone. Was it bad that the person who knew me best was an employee?

With a last look at the cottage and the man now silhouetted against the window, I turned to my fun evening of paperwork.

Chapter 11

I threw the papers onto the table in frustration. I'd been at this for hours and nothing. The numbers all tied back. The projects all seemed legit. What the dzrak was Vass thinking wasting my time with this? I had a good mind to call him up, even if it was midnight. I pinched the bridge of my nose and pushed my phone away. Venting wouldn't do any good. It would more than likely get me another pile of paper hand-delivered by a grumpy harpy. I began shuffling the papers into a stack instead. I needed some sleep and a fresh take on all this.

As I was stacking the paper, a name caught my eye. The Director. So high up in the organisation that was literally how he signed his name. Egotistical? Maybe. Protecting his identity? Definitely. A thought occurred to me. Did I actually know who he was? I'd seen him a handful of times when I was working at the London branch. A tall figure with tanned skin and a slick haircut. He wore dark glasses. That was an avenue to research. I scribbled a note to myself on my phone.

My eyes drifted pack to his signature and I pulled the paper out of the pile. It was the project that allowed the Office to communicate with supernaturals in their sleep. Interesting. I scanned the summary. It had been in progress for years. There were various permissions for testing attached to the report. Different magical beings and even some mundane ones had been used. I wasn't surprised to see wyrms on that list, they were said to be distant evolutionary cousins to dragons and now I knew it had all been a ruse to wake up a giant lizard that all made sense.

On instinct I rifled through the papers again, pulling out everything with the Director's signature on it. I stared at the projects he had personally signed off on: Portal technology to replicate magic users' abilities and sustain portals for longer, Draconic language studies, weapons forging, Fae realms, even my own taskforce was there. I narrowed my eyes at one report that seemed to be about a doomsday weapon.

I rubbed my eyes. If there was a pattern there, I couldn't see it. I gave up for the night and settled into my camp bed. I pulled a thin blanket over myself and drifted to sleep. Dragons and portals filled my mind.

I woke up with the sunrise after a couple of hours sleep. I ducked into the kitchen as the jackdaw flew at me. I swore at it and filled up my small kettle before I made myself a strong coffee. I had left the good coffee in the guest house. My nose told me I wouldn't enjoy the cup of brown water I was brewing. I tried it anyway before grimacing and throwing it down the sink. I'd have to get myself a ration from the cottage later. I downed a glass of water instead and headed out for a run. My thoughts turned to running with Mum across these hills. In our lynx forms, we would prowl through the night. I could still remember her disappointment when I gave in to my animal instincts and killed a sheep in my enthusiasm. *"We don't need to draw attention to ourselves. If you want to hunt, stick to rabbits and small game. I can't lose you like your father."* She was right. The rumours of wild mountain lions had gone into overdrive when they found the carcass. She hadn't allowed us to shift until the next full moon forced our change and even then we had to stay inside the barn. I shook my head as if that would get rid of painful memories. I stayed in my human form, thankful it was still early in the lunar cycle. I didn't need another clash with big cat hunters.

I waved a greeting to Dick as I jogged back towards my home. He was stretching outside, a cup of coffee in one hand. The aroma floated towards me on the soft breeze. I needed to get some of the good beans.

I hand a wash in the sink and got changed out of my workout clothes before returning to staring at paperwork until Sam arrived at nine on the dot. I loved his punctuality.

"Hi there!"

"Morning, this is Dick," I introduced my renter as he strolled over, "He's staying here for a while and has offered to help out."

Sam sized him up then held out his hand. They shook for a while and I snorted in annoyance at the alpha male dominance that seemed to be going on. I didn't need that drama.

"Before we get started, Claire said to tell you that she wants to have dinner tonight round ours."

"I'm not really sure…"

"She said she wasn't taking no for an answer and she'd come here and cook if that's easier."

"Tonight sounds great."

"Good, well I'll tell her." He turned to Dick, "You're invited too."

"I'd love to. If her cooking is as good as her bakery, I'm looking forward to tonight," Dick's acceptance was a lot more gracious than mine had been.

Sam beamed at the compliment to his wife, "You're in for a treat, I tell you. Now, let's see what we've got here." The builder rubbed his hands together and we trooped upstairs. He took one look at the pipe work, complimented Dick on an effective seal and then laid out his plan of attack.

"First thing is to fix this and get that shower back on. It's pretty old so I might need to get a new one, but we'll cross that bridge when we get to it. While I'm doing that, it's best to weatherproof what we can. I've brought tarps and ply board so can you two start battening down the hatches and getting those windows sealed up. You'll need to have one large bit of ply over the spongy floor in the small room, I don't want anyone falling through. Tomorrow, the real work will begin!" With that, the squat builder knelt down and began to hum a tuneless melody as he got to work.

I met Dick's chocolate brown eyes. He shrugged and gestured for me to lead the way, "Ladies first."

I narrowed my eyes then marched out of the door. I hated that chivalrous bull schiztz. I led the way outside and heaved a large piece of pressed wood from the back of the van.

"Wow, you mind givin' me your work out tips?!" Dick was staring at me as he pulled on some heavy duty gloves to protect his hands from splinters. Dzrak. I did not want to draw attention to myself. I decided to style it out.

"Running mostly, kickboxing…that sort of thing." How could I put my Magical Liaison Office training into a few words? It had taken months of all sorts of physical training plus the knowledge tests.

"I've done a bit of jiu jitsu in my time, but hey whatever you're doin' it's working," he struggled to lift his own board. I shook my head and left him to it. He was halfway to the door when I made it back outside.

"A little help?"

I was impressed. In my experience, males of any species didn't usually ask for help. I grabbed one end and we manoeuvred it through the doorway together. I was leading the way and took us to the kitchen. The dzraking jackdaw dive-bombed me. I swore and hefted the wood up as a shield. The bird stopped just in time and settled on the fridge croaking at us angrily.

"What was that you said?"

"What? Dzrak?"

"What language is that?"

"Dwarfish. It's a dzraking great language for swearing in."

"It sounds it, I'll have to remember that…Dzrak" I heard him muttering the word to himself a few times while he got his tongue around it. Somehow he gave the harsh word a husky flavour, a lot more attractive than the times I'd heard it shouted out in the middle of a brawl.

The house was already in such a state there didn't seem much point trying to keep any mess outside so we brought in Sam's saw and carved up the boards to match the window size in the kitchen. I was about to shoo the bird out when Dick stopped me.

"Hadn't we better check it doesn't have chicks in there first?" He was already taking a step towards the chimney where it had made its home.

"It doesn't."

"How can you be so sure?"

"I checked yesterday, but please, be my guest." I hadn't checked but my sensitive ears hadn't picked up any cheeping and it was late for a bird to have eggs. If he wanted to check out a musty chimney, that was fine by me. The jackdaw eyed him beadily. I crossed my arms and leant against the worn sides. Dick crouched down and reached his hand into the chimney. I saw him grimace as he felt through years of dust, twigs and piles of bird guano. The stale stench of it hit me and I was glad the window was open.

"No babies or eggs," he confirmed after a few minutes, "shall I pull it all out?"

"Go for it." I took a step backwards out of the kitchen while he pulled handfuls of debris from the chimneybreast.

The jackdaw cawed throatily and flew to attack the human messing up its home. The bird scratched its clawed feet along Dick's back. He screamed in alarm. I gave a menacing growl, allowing it to rumble in my chest. The bird flew up in fear. I flapped my arms at it and got it out of the window. Clouds of dust and dirt were falling from the chimney. I edged out of the room, sneezing. Once the noise of falling sticks had finished I counted to ten before looking in. I didn't see him at first. Then a pile of dust moved and shook itself off. His brown hair was peppered grey and white and his clothes were covered in grimy powder.

"Well dzrak!" he swore.

I bit my lip, trying to stop myself from laughing. It didn't work. "I'll go find a towel," I managed between fits of giggles. His own eyes crinkled in amusement as he shook the dust from his hair. He saw me stepping away from the dirt and moved towards me.

"Let's see how funny it is when you're covered in bird poop!"

I batted him away and jogged out of the door. I heard him laughing at my flight. Maybe I did need to loosen up. I spotted a hose near the door. That gave me an idea. Grinning at the prank I had in mind, I spent a couple of minutes setting everything up before I headed over to the guest house.

Humming to myself I made a round of hot drinks, grabbed a towel and some cleaning equipment before heading back. Dick and Sam were grateful to gulp down the hot coffee and remove the dust that had settled in everyone's throats. We got back to work. I went to saw off the branch that had claimed my old bedroom and left Dick downstairs to sort out the mess he'd made in the kitchen. I smirked when I heard his squeal after Sam turned the water on just before lunch.

"Sonofa…"

I walked downstairs as nonchalantly as I could, "Something wrong?"

"Was this you?"

"I don't know what you're talking about," I tried to keep a straight face. I had set the hose up to blast through the window as soon as there was water pressure. From the looks of it, a jet of water had hit Dick right in the face before he'd jumped out of the way. Now water was pouring into the room, creating brown puddles where it hit the filth. I walked out to turn it off. Dick greeted me at the side of the house, now holding the green hose pipe. He must have used the back door.

"Put 'em up!" his phony cowboy accent was awful.

"Easy there…" I held my hands up, backing away slowly.

He aimed the stream of water. I leapt to one side. He angled it to follow me. I couldn't keep dodging the jet of water so I ran towards him. He took great pleasure in soaking me until I was close enough to wrestle it off him. With a cry of triumph, I wrested the hosepipe free and turned it on my attacker. He burbled something as the water hit him in the face. Then we were both laughing. He managed to duck under the fountain of water and gripped my wrists. His grasp was strong and I let him force the hose down towards the ground.

"Truce?" I asked.

He pushed a stray lock of wet hair behind my ear. I gazed into his warm eyes, suddenly aware of how close we were. His face had been washed clean from the water and a drop of water ran down his face and disappeared underneath his neckline. I had the urge to lick it up. His t-shirt was clinging wetly to his muscled chest, leaving nothing to the imagination. I trembled slightly in my desire. The vampire was right, it had been too long if all it took was a wet t-shirt to get me hot and bothered.

"Are you cold?" his voice was full of concern. I shook my head, not sure where my power of speech had gone. I tilted my face upwards and pressed into him.

"Hey! I thought I said we needed to waterproof this place, not waterlog it!" Sam's voice cut through the intimate moment. I jumped backwards, putting distance between me and Dick. I twisted the hose's nozzle closed as Sam came round the corner. He was wiping his hands on a rag and it took him a moment to focus on us.

"We were just…getting cleaned up." It was a weak excuse. The hose was still dripping in my hand.

The lopsided grin on Sam's face told me he didn't believe a word, "Sure, well you two might want to get changed out of those wet things. I'm going to get some lunch, when I get back I'll go see how bad the roof is." He walked off, still wiping his hands on the torn cloth.

I walked over to the outside tap and turned the water off at the source. "Right, well I'll see you after lunch."

"We could eat together?"

It was tempting. That’s why I had to refuse, “No thanks, I’d better check up on my reports if I don’t want another late night tonight.”

“Are they going somewhere?”

I smiled weakly and headed inside.

The rest of the afternoon passed awkwardly. I carried on hacking away at the tree that was growing inside the house, using my pent up energy to saw the wood. Sam commandeered Dick into holding his ladder so he could check the roof. The prognosis wasn’t good. The whole thing was going to have to come off and be re-laid. The builder tacked a plastic tarpaulin across the hole so it was a bit more waterproof. At about three o’ clock he found me sitting astride the tree, still trimming it back. I stepped down and walked with him downstairs.

“I’m off then, got to get some shopping and get ready for tonight. See you later.”

I waved him off and was about to get back to work. I turned at the sound of another footstep in the hall. Dick.

“I, er, thought I might go for a walk while the sun’s out.”

I sniffed the air, “Careful, there’s a storm coming in. I’d say you’ve got about an hour and I can’t be held responsible for what Claire might do if we’re late!”

He grinned at me, glad I’d broken the tension and headed off for his walk. I caught him looking up at the clear blue sky in disbelief. I shook my head behind him as I headed back upstairs. Storms roll in fast on the hills. The darkening light as I worked in the small bedroom proved me right. Before long I could hear the raindrops hitting the plastic sheet on the roof. When the rain started pelting me through the leaves, I decided to tack up my own tarpaulin and call it a day.

I was going through the reports, still puzzling about the connection between the research, if there was any, when another name caught my eye. Vass had a countersignature on one of the projects. Was it a coincidence he had signed off on my taskforce and our expedition to Stonehenge and Avebury as well? He'd said he'd been on the Director's case for a while, maybe it was a deliberate ploy to get me involved. I could feel a tension headache coming on from the thoughts swirling through my head and the storm building overhead. I pinched the bridge of my nose, annoyed at myself for not understanding any of it. I texted Maxi to see if he had found anything, annoyed that I could be playing right into the Director's hands. Dzrak I hated politics. Maybe Dot was right, I should take it easy and give myself a break. My thoughts turned treacherously towards a certain someone staying just a few paces away in the small cottage. A smile curled onto my lips as I thought about us being caught in the rain together, picking up where we'd left off under the hosepipe.

As the first rumble of thunder exploded overhead, I realised I hadn't heard Dick come back in. Hoping I was mistaken, I sprinted over to the guest house. I stood on the doorstep knocking. This was going to take some explaining if he had made it back in time. I pushed my discomfort down and knocked again. Nothing. I checked the window like a stalker. No one was in the open plan kitchen or sitting area. He was still out there in the storm.

Chapter 12

I tilted my head, reaching out with my senses. There was a faint trace of his scent: leather mixed with cedar wood and a hint of paper, but the downpour made it hard to pinpoint. I squinted my eyes against the rain and tried to pick out his footprints in the mud. It was no good. I couldn't see anything through the sheets of water. I caught sight of Patches pacing nervously under the iron steps. I picked her up and let her inside with my spare key, "Don't worry girl, I'll find him."

I pinched the bridge of my nose in frustration. I would have to shift to have any hope of finding my missing house guest. I looked around warily, checking I was alone in the dark storm before making the change.

In my large lynx form, I shook my heavy fur coat instinctively against the rain then gave up. The Welsh weather was relentless. In this form, my senses stretched out into the storm. The rain pounded loudly against the hard ground. My eyes picked out a rabbit dashing for cover under a hedge. I resisted the urge to chase it. Instead I descended the iron steps and sniffed the ground. Dick's scent was still faint but, as a lynx, I could trace it.

I padded after him, tracing his steps along the footpath. I moved quickly, my large paws hitting the ground and splattering mud up my coppery coat. I was going to need a shower after this. I gave a shake against the rain and kept going. A bolt of lightning split the sky. It illuminated the mountains sharply. Rocks cast dark shadows against the grass. Thunder swiftly followed, echoing around the land. My ears flattened against my head in protest against the noise. I shook my head, forcing myself to keep going. The mountain wasn't the place to be in a storm. Thoughts of Dick lost, maybe injured, filled my mind. I continued onwards. The rain was turning the dirt track into a small stream. I tried to walk on one side but the newly made mud slid wetly under my paws. I cursed inwardly. Outwardly I let out a soft growl of frustration. At the top of the mountain track I paused. His scent was gone. I turned my head left and right, inhaling deeply. Raindrops trickled down the side of my muzzle. Nothing. I scanned the ground, searching for a footprint or anything that would help me locate him. Great. The storm had washed away any trace of the man. Fighting my growing anxiety that he was lost, I decided he had stuck to the path and moved forwards.

Less than five minutes later, I stopped again. The path split into two, stretching across the fields in either direction. I stood at the top and stared futilely into the storm. Any animals here had long since found shelter. I was alone. Another bolt of lightning crackled down, lighting up the sky. Something caught my eye. A splash of white in the dark field. I walked over cautiously as thunder filled my ears, keeping low to the ground. As I approached, Dick's scent filled my nose accompanied by the overwhelming sweetness of sugar and cacao. A chocolate wrapper. It must have blown from his grasp. I lifted my head and felt the wind hit my face. If the wind had taken it, my best guess was that Dick was ahead of me somewhere. Heading against the wind, I moved on. I went more slowly now, turning my head to look at every tree and bush in case Dick was sheltering somewhere.

The next flash of lightning showed me what I was looking for. A boot sticking out from behind a craggy, grey rock. At least he wasn't hiding underneath a tall tree in a lightning storm. I padded over quickly then paused. Best to see what state he was in before deciding what to do. I leaped soundlessly onto the rock and climbed up then lay down. The hard, wet stone, was warm against my belly as I inched forward. At the edge, I peered down. Dick was there, huddled under a slight overhang. His arms were wrapped around his knees as he tried to keep warm in the storm. Water was pooled around him, still dripping from his clothes. Great. The temperature was still warm on the summer's day, but it was still easy to catch a chill and get seriously ill when you were soaked. I hesitated for a moment then jumped down.

His head snapped up as he heard my landing. I was graceful, but I was still a couple of hundred pounds of large cat landing on wet ground straight in front of him. It didn't help that my landing coincided with another streak of lighting and a simultaneous roll of thunder. I hadn't intended to have such a dramatic entrance. He let out a cry of fear and surprise before getting his reaction under control. He tried to back away, arms and legs scrabbling frantically, but he was already against the rock. I sat down, ignoring the mud squelching under me. I had to make him think I wasn't a threat.

"Er, shoo! Go on! Please don't eat me! I won't taste good!"

I rolled my eyes at his protests. He stopped talking. His eyes darted to the left. He began edging along the rock face. He was thinking of making a run for it back into the storm.

I sighed. It came out like a snort from deep in my throat. I couldn't let him go out into the storm again. With another snorty sigh, I lay down on the wet ground. Something no predator on the hunt would do. The sodden grass pressed into my stomach. It was uncomfortable and very wet. He stopped moving, his eyes watching me carefully. I inched my way forward, keeping my amber eyes locked on his deep brown ones. I ended up at his side, blocking him from making a run the way he was thinking. He was rigid with tension, I could smell it oozing from him, but he stayed still. I stood and turned in a circle, trying to find a comfortable spot before curling up next to him. I deliberately allowed my side to touch his thigh, providing comfort and warmth in the hostile weather. I laid my head on my paws and closed my eyes. It looked like we were waiting out the storm here. After a while, I felt the tension leave him. He relaxed enough to start moving his hand over his knee towards my head. I adjusted my position slightly and slitted my eyes open, watching him.

"Hey there, guess we're waiting out the weather here together huh? Where did you come from I wonder? Are you the dangerous mountain lion they talk about in town?" His hand continued to edge over his thigh. When he reached out his little finger to 'accidentally' brush my head, I sat up quickly and shook myself. Beads of water left my thick coat and landed on him. He lifted his arm to cover his eyes and laughed. The sound connected somewhere inside my stomach, causing a warm heat to spread through me. Acting on instinct I nuzzled his cheek, marking him with my own animal scent. I felt our scents combine. It smelled right somehow. I sat back on my haunches and considered him. Then I shook my head again. What was I doing? Acting like he was my mate? Not likely. I didn't have time for that anyway. I looked away from his eyes filled with a combination of humour and wonder and settled back next to him. I told myself that the only reason I was lying so close to him was the need to keep him warm. It was nothing to do with that swirling feeling in the pit of my stomach, or the intoxicating aroma of his unique scent. Great. Now things were getting really complicated.

The storm passed quickly enough, a typical summer tempest. The prickly feeling I had in any thunderstorm quieted inside me. The sky lightened as the clouds hastened away, moving on to the next town. As soon as the rain stopped, I stood. We had to get moving. I stepped out from under the rock and gave my coat another shake. This time far enough away that he only got a sprinkling.

"Nice to meet you cat, I'll see you around…if I can find my way home."

Home. The word sounded right on his lips. But I couldn't let him get lost. I huffed out a sigh and sat down, cocking my head to one side.

"Not going anywhere huh? Well I can wait all day."

I rolled my eyes and took three steps away towards the path, then looked back over my shoulder and motioned with my head for him to follow me.

"If I didn't know better, I'd say you were showing me the way home…" wonderment filled his deep voice.

I made the motion again. I couldn't make it much clearer.

"Alright then, I'll follow you. I guess it'll make a good story. Just don't kill me OK?"

I snorted at his concern that I might kill him, although if he didn't hurry up, I might be tempted to drag him. I motioned with my head for a third time and carried on, picking my way carefully to give him the best ground to walk on. Partway down the slippery path, he fell, going over hard on his ankle. I heard him swear as he hit the ground. Great. I hadn't heard the bone break but a twisted ankle was still painful to walk on. I padded over to inspect it. I opened my mouth to lift his jeans. He got the wrong idea, seeing my sharp teeth bared and balled his hand into a fist. His punch connected hard with the side of my head. I snarled and backed out of his reach. He was trying to push himself upwards. I shook myself and regarded him.

"Easy now, I don't want to hurt you and I don't want you to hurt me." Idiot. As if he could actually injure a full-grown shifter. If I wanted to hurt him, he'd be crying out in pain by now, but I wasn't going to let that punch go unrewarded. Unsurprisingly, he slipped again and landed hard on his backside. In two leaps, I was behind him. My jaw closed on his shoulder. He yelped. I pulled him up the path to a section where there was less mud. I upped the pressure slightly before I let go, allowing him to feel my canines and my power. The thought crossed my mind that if we were a mated pair, a bite would claim him for my own. I let go quickly, not wanting to explore that line of thought.

“Er thanks,” he pushed himself upwards and rubbed his shoulder. There might be a bruise there but nothing serious. He winced as he placed pressure on his ankle. Great. We were still a long way from the house. There was no way he was going to make it without help. With another huff of resignation, I pressed against him and forced my head under his hand.

“You want me to lean on you?” his voice was cautious. I nudged his hand again then moved forwards so it rested on my shoulders. Lucky that I was tall enough to lend him some support in this form. It was slow going along the treacherous path. He slipped again a couple of times, but I leaned my weight into his to prevent him tumbling over. The sun was bright in the sky and birds chirped merrily as we arrived back to the edge of my property. He was panting from the exertion of walking down a mountain with a twisted ankle and leant on the fence to catch his breath. I took the opportunity to slink off.

“Wait, you’re going?”

I turned back to face him.

“Well, thank you…” he met my eyes and nodded with understanding, as if he realised that I wasn’t all that I seemed. That warm feeling flushed through me again. How long had it been since I’d allowed anyone to understand me and accept my dual nature? I turned away and trotted alongside the fence. He had no idea it was me, his landlady; he thought I was a dumb animal who had helped him out. I ducked through a gap in the wooden fence and kept to the shadows as I found somewhere out of sight to shift. A flash across the fields caught my attention. Something was glinting in the sunlight. Metal? Or glass? I narrowed my eyes. Was someone watching my farm?

A cry brought my attention back to the injured man.

Chapter 13

Ducking behind a tree, I shifted quickly back to my human form and ran towards the cry. I skidded to a halt as I approached Dick. I took in the scene. He had tried to climb the fence and was now stuck on top of the wooden beam, his t-shirt snagged by a rogue nail.

I met his embarrassed gaze.

"Well look what the cat dragged in," I couldn't help myself.

"Funny you should say that, you're not gonna believe what just happened! Er, a little help?"

With a sigh, I moved forward and unhooked his t-shirt. Then I wrapped an arm around his back and braced to take his weight and help him down. He leaned on me gratefully as he descended. I caught the slight wince as he tested his ankle on the ground. This close his musky scent filled my nostrils, mingling with the sweet smell of earth after a storm. It was a heady combination. I couldn't move away and offered to support him to his house. He nodded, concentrating on breathing through the pain. I was grateful he was focused on walking and not talking about his unlikely rescue. I wasn't sure how I could react in a believable way. We made slow but steady progress over the uneven gravel. After an awkward manoeuvre up the steps, we were inside the small cottage. Patches instantly began winding herself around our feet. I moved her tactfully out of the way with one of my boots before we tripped. I helped him over to the neat, small sofa and settled him down. The small cat jumped up onto his lap and began licking his face. I frowned. For some stupid reason, I felt a little jealous of the cat showing him affection.

Seeing he was looking at me, I switched my frown to his foot and gestured to his ankle, "I should take a look at that."

He nodded his agreement and I untied his boot before rolling down his black, cotton sock. At least he'd been wearing sensible walking gear. I pressed gently around his ankle, studying his face carefully for a reaction. He was trying to hide his pain, but not succeeding.

"How does it feel?"

"Flippin' painful!"

"Can you move it?"

He humoured me by rotating his foot slowly then flapping it up and down. Nothing broken.

"Looks like you twisted it. I'll cancel our dinner plans."

He sat upright, "No way! I want to meet your friends. I'm fine, I just need to walk it off."

I gave him a look that said I didn't believe a word.

"Seriously, I'm fine. I just need a shower and then I'll strap it back in my boot for support."

"I'll leave you to it then. I'll come and get you in half an hour, you'll need help getting down those steps."

He started to protest then conceded the point and shrugged before beginning to peel off his other boot. Him removing clothes was my cue to leave. I headed to the door.

"Hey, how come you're soaked?" He'd clocked my wet clothes and hair and was looking at me curiously.

It was my turn to shrug, "I went looking for you in case you were lost…I guess I must have chosen the wrong path." It was close to the truth and, with a smile, I was gone before he could press me further.

Half an hour and a change of clothes later, I was back at his door. I gave a knock and heard him shout that I should come in. I opened the door and stepped in, unconsciously inhaling his male scent.

"Are you ready?"

"Nearly," he stepped out of his bedroom, pulling a clean t-shirt over his muscled chest. I wondered how he worked out to get those abs before flicking my gaze upwards.

"Hey, I wanted to say thank you. Without you and that cat, I wouldn't have made it home."

As if on cue, Patches strolled in through the open door. She sniffed my foot delicately then sashayed over to Dick. She wound her body through his legs before heading into his bedroom. He bent down and picked her up easily.

“Not so fast little one. We had an agreement: you sleep on the couch,” he put her down carefully on a cushion. She meowed but it was a half-hearted protest and she curled up happily. I envied her.

“Right, shall we get a move on?” I gestured towards the door.

He smiled and hobbled over, using the furniture and then the kitchen countertops as props. He stood next to me, close and male. I took a deep breath, fighting back my impulse to stay in tonight. Instead, I offered him my arm and braced myself to support him down the steps.

“We should take a gift.” Another person obsessed with hospitality. I looked around the sparse kitchen and snagged the second bottle of wine I had left as a welcoming present for him.

“How’s this?”

“Perfect.”

“Great. Let’s go.”

He allowed me to help him down the steps and towards the car. “Who’s driving?” he joked. I gave him a look and opened the door for him.

“I could get used to being chauffeured about.”

“Not likely!” I snorted as I slammed the door shut. The chuckle on his lips told me he had heard me. Great. I was coming across as angry and impatient. I mean, I was both of those things, but I wanted him to like me.

I drove quickly to the outskirts of the town. Dick was gracious enough not to grab the 'oh shit' handle above the car door, but I saw his hands tense on his knees.

"I'll have to give you a ride some time. The scenery looks even better on a bike."

I glanced across. He looked genuine but then he turned his gaze out of the window, taking in the lowering sun and the golden rays peppering the mountains from between fluffy clouds. Only the puddles filling the potholes showed any indication there had been a storm earlier.

As we entered the town, I slowed and got Dick to read me the instructions in Claire's text. There weren't many houses and we found hers soon enough. I parked up outside the square, redbrick new build. There were a couple of hanging baskets framing the door, overflowing with purple trumpets and trailing ivy. Claire made a good home. I caught a whiff of food and smoke. She made a good dinner too. I helped Dick out and acted as his crutch up to the white front door.

I rapped smartly on the door with my knuckles. Claire opened the door almost instantly. A frilly pink apron was fastened around her waist and a wisp of flour clung to her low bun.

"Welcome, welcome, come in," she ushered us in before shouting over her shoulder, "They're here!"

"What happened to you?" a small voice came down the stairs. I looked up. A child's face was peeking out between the bannisters.

"I fell," replied Dick easily.

"Go on, off to bed with you! I told you we've got company! If you're good, I'll save you some pudding. Now scoot!" Claire hurried upstairs to help her child to bed, "Go on through, Sam's in the garden."

I followed the direction of the smoke and helped Dick into a neat, rectangular garden lined with trimmed flowerbeds. Sam was standing on the patio, frantically moving burgers and sausages from a hot barbeque to a plate. He stopped as he saw us.

"Glad you could make it! I was getting worried, what with the storm and everything. It's lucky we could have a barbeque. Can I get you a drink?" he gestured to a cooler brimming with icy water. Bottles of beer and cider were bobbing in it, keeping cool. I helped Dick into a chair and exchanged the bottle of wine for two beers. I twisted the tops off effortlessly and handed one to Dick.

"Blimey Ruth, those aren't screwtops!" Sam was staring at the beers in my hands.

"Right…it's an old trick."

"Wish I knew tricks that came in as handy as that!" With a flourish, Sam placed the plate of well-done meat onto the table next to bread buns. Claire came bustling out of the kitchen through the bi-fold doors, carrying a bowl of leafy salad and some bottles of sauce.

"Ta-da! Dinner is served!"

We tucked in.

"So, what happened to your ankle then?" Claire pointed at Dick's outstretched leg with her fork.

"Well I went for a walk up the mountain, then the storm came in…but that's not the crazy part. I was sheltering under this rock when a giant cat came up and sat next to me. It's the darnedest thing. She waited with me during the storm and then, you're not gonna believe this, but she led me back to Ruth's place. It was really weird but I got the feeling she knew me somehow," he ended by shaking his head and taking another sip of his beer.

Claire and Sam exchanged glances. "Well, you've met our mountain lion then. There's many stories about that lion helping those who get lost in the mountains…not so much nowadays, but still. There's those who think it's a myth see, but I saw it once too."

I rolled my eyes as Claire launched into a story about how she wandered off one day and got hopelessly lost. The 'lion' had led her back to her Mum. I smiled inwardly. I remembered that day well. It had been cloudy with the smell of rain in the air. Her Mum had been frantic with worry as the spring day turned to night and called everyone who lived near the mountain to help find her. I had bolted off immediately to find my friend before a search party could form. My Mum hadn't even been too angry when she found out what had happened. *Just promise me you'll be careful when you shift*, *I can't lose you too* had been her only reprimand.

"What about you? You live right up by the mountain, you must have seen it too." All eyes turned to me. I chewed a mouthful of meat while I considered.

"I don't know what to tell you, I've never seen it on the mountain." That was true. I'd need a mirror to see myself.

"What kind of a cat do you think it is?"

I listened while they discussed my shifter form, listing everything from cougars to jaguars.

"The tufty ears it had though, it kind of reminded me of a lynx."

I spluttered on my drink as Dick named my true form. It was the first time anyone had identified me correctly. They turned to me with concern and Claire slapped me on the back a few times as I recovered.

"So, wild cats aside, what are you doing in these hills, Dick?"

"I'm hoping to get some inspiration actually, away from the hustle and bustle of city life."

"Inspiration? What do you do?" Claire was intrigued.

"I'm a writer."

"Oh, what do you write? I love to read, maybe I've heard of you?"

"A bit of fantasy really."

"That's cool, I love Doctor Who myself, never miss an episode!" Sam chimed in. As he began listing the merits of each Doctor in turn, Claire suddenly pushed her chair back and rushed back inside. I frowned after her but, judging from the sweet aroma wafting our way, she was just worried about her dessert getting burned.

Sam had reached Doctor number six and the sun had started to dip below the horizon, when Claire came back out brandishing a cake and a book triumphantly.

“I knew I recognised you from somewhere!” She placed the chocolate cake onto the table carefully then turned the book over. Staring at us from the back cover was Dick! I reached for the book and read the title: *Lovers Reunion in Elfwood*. Beneath the large font, a topless male held a woman with pointy ears and not much clothing in a swooning embrace. The author’s name was R Derson. Not much of a stretch for a pen name there.

“I love your books, Renald is my favourite character – how did you come up with such amazing story lines?” Claire gushed, “Oh My G! Are you here writing your latest novel? What’s going to happen to Sheri?”

I flipped the book over and scanned the blurb on the back. It promised steamy romance in the heart of the elven lands. Not my usual read, but I guessed it was popular if Claire was so excited about it.

“Now, now dear, leave the author alone,” Sam placed his hand on his wife’s arm.

Claire took a deep breath, “You’re right, sorry. Who’s for cake?”

“Hey, it’s OK. I love knowing that people like my characters, but I don’t want to spoil the twist ending for you. Let me just say that things aren’t always what they seem!”

Claire’s eyes widened. Sam took the knife from her and dished up the dessert.

“At least sign something for me? I’ll get a pen!”

With a flourish, Dick took the proffered pen and signed the paperback. Claire hugged it to her chest.

As Sam began clearing the dishes, I asked Claire, “Could I borrow that?”

“Oh well if you haven’t read any of Derson’s work before, you really should start at the beginning of the series. I’ll get it for you.”

“Why?” Dick waited until Claire was gone to speak. His voice sounded accusatory to my ears.

Annoyed, I frowned at him, “Maybe I want to read a good book. Maybe I want to find out more about my mysterious house guest.”

He leaned back in his chair, “I’m an open book, you can ask me anything.”

Claire returned before I could reply, carrying three thick paperbacks. Their creased spines and yellowing pages told me she’d read them many times. She always was a romantic.

“Thanks.”

She waved off my appreciation and our compliments over the meal as we chatted. Soon enough, I noticed the tired lines around Dick’s eyes and decided it was time to leave. I drove along roads made golden by the setting sun.

“I meant it you know,” Dick’s voice was low and intense in the confined space of my car. I shot him a questioning look. “I’m an open book, you can ask me anything.”

“Hmmm…” I pretended to think, “do you prefer Coca Cola or Pepsi?”

He let out a snort of laughter, “Pepsi I guess, but my favourite soft drink is lemonade. You?”

"Cool water for me."

"Huh, figures."

"What do you mean?" I bristled.

"Nothing. I just figured you for someone who plays by the rules, prizes honesty and likes to keep things on the straight and narrow. Makes sense you'd choose water."

"What does that mean? Are you trying to turn me into one of your characters?" I was annoyed he'd summed me up so neatly.

He smiled at that, "No, if you were one of my characters, we wouldn't be talking so much."

"What would we be doing?" He tucked a stray hair behind my ear. I leaned into his touch without thinking. "Why do you write that stuff?" I killed the mood quickly.

"That 'stuff' lets people escape into a world of happy endings most of us don't have the luxury to live in."

"When you put it like that, I can see the appeal."

"What's your story?"

"You first Mr open book."

"Not much to tell. Thought I found the love of my life. Followed her to the States. Turns out she wasn't who I thought she was and after the second time she cheated on me, I finally found the balls to walk out. But I lost my muse. Now I'm trying to find out who I am without her. I'm hoping that a change of scenery will help me pick up the pen on my novels again."

I reached my hand over to his, "I'm sorry."

"Don't be. It's better this way. Better to be out of it than living a lie. So, what's your story?"

I shrugged and pulled my hand away back to the steering wheel. "If I tell you, will you put me in one of your books?" I joked.

"Maybe, but I'll change your name, how about that?" he saw my face darken at the memories piled up inside me. "Sorry, I overreach sometimes. Don't worry, you don't have to tell me."

I gripped the steering wheel harder. Might as well say it out loud. "Dad was killed. Mum got cancer. She didn't make it. So I guess I'm all alone apart from the job. Sad huh?"

"Yeah," he reached for my hand this time and I let him hold it. The weight on my chest seemed to ease a little at sharing my burden. I pulled into the driveway and parked up. I turned to face him. My eyes flicked to his lips then met his eyes. I decided not to think for once and let instinct guide me. I leaned forward. A gunshot cracked through the air.

Chapter 14

I was out of the car in a second, scanning my driveway for the source of the blast. It had sounded so close that it could have come from anywhere. I couldn't see anything and ran over to Dick's side of the car. Something felt off, but I couldn't place it. I turned my head, relying on my sense of smell. The wind was picking up, blowing from behind the car. All I could get was the whiff of the car's exhaust and the grassy smell from the fields behind us. Whoever it was had picked a spot downwind. Dick was already trying to get out of the car, swearing under his breath as his ankle was still sore.

I moved to his side and propped him up and we instinctively headed towards the smaller cottage. We were halfway across the drive when the van headlights lit us up. Instantly I knew what had felt wrong. The van had been turned around, ready to make a quick getaway…or run us over.

"Stop right there!"

I squinted against the light, “Billy, is that you?”

The scruffy man stepped forward to the edge of the light, cradling a shot gun between his hands. “You’ve been keeping a secret from us.”

“I don’t know what you’re talking about! Now leave before I call the police again!” I moved my hand towards my handbag

“Oh, I don’t think you’ll be doing that.” He aimed the gun directly at us. I could probably survive, but Dick was human. I didn’t like where this was going.

“OK, OK, calm down. This is between us, let me take Dick back to the house and we can talk, just you and me.”

His friend stepped into the light. I almost groaned at the caption on his top: *I’m not a gynacologist, but I’ll take a look*. Gynaecologist was spelled incorrectly. He aimed his gun in our direction too. I caught the wisp of smoke above the barrel. So he was the one who had fired. I wondered if it had been an accident.

“We can talk just fine here. Now show me the lion!”

“What?”

“Don’t play dumb! We saw it come back here this afternoon, then it disappeared. I’m not stupid, I know you’ve got something to do with it. Tell me where it is and we’ll leave you alone.”

“What are you going to do with it?” I was trying to buy some time while I thought of a plan. I briefly considered shifting, but the man at my side made me think again. He had been accepting when I was a lynx, sure, but seeing someone change shape is not a pleasant experience and I was worried he'd reject me. I didn't know why I cared so much, but I did.

"I think its head will look really nice on my wall! Don't make me ask again!"

"Look, I…" I didn't get any further before he fired his gun into the ground in front of us. I pulled us back instinctively.

My eyes flicked from one to the other. If I was right, both had one cartridge left before they'd have to reload. How could I use that?

"You got something to say?" he asked again, adjusting his aim.

I was looking at his friend, he was aiming at me and I didn't like how his finger was trembling. I guessed he'd been brought along for the ride and hadn't realised it would go so far.

"You don't want to do this," I spoke to slogan t-shirt, trying to reach through the fear. I side stepped forwards in front of Dick. Before I could say anything else, Dick pushed me roughly down. Off balance, I hit the floor and rolled onto my side.

"Where I'm from, we don't talk to ladies like that!" He had both of their attention now. I fought back my irritation at him treating me like a damsel in distress and planned my move. I positioned myself into a crouch and began to shuffle along the ground slowly. If I could take out Billy, his mate would back off. I knew how idiot human so-called alphas worked.

A flicker of movement caught my eye from the other side of the van. I heard the trigger click. I reacted instantly. I shifted as I leapt to push Dick out of the way. Faced with a couple of hundred pounds of muscled lynx, he crumpled. I felt a flash of pain in my shoulder as we went down. I heard his exhale of breath as the impact with the ground winded him.

Slogan t-shirt pissed himself. Again. He dropped his gun, turned and fled, running back towards the road.

Billy stood there in shock, "You…how?"

I pulled myself off Dick and faced him, keeping my foreleg off the ground. A low growl rumbled from my throat. I bared my teeth. I wasn't done yet. I heard Dick groaning as he recovered from the fall. He was moving to the side, away from us. Good. I took a step towards Billy, growling at the pain that shot through my shoulder. I forced myself forwards.

He swung the gun back up to aim at me. I didn't know how good a shot he was, but at this range, he didn't need to be. I tensed. I'd have one shot at this. Pun intended.

My ears pricked as a gun cocked to my right. Billy hadn't noticed. Great. Was slogan back? I risked a glance to the source of the noise. Dick. He had picked up the discarded weapon and reloaded it. Now he was aiming it at Billy.

"Back off!"

Billy ignored him and continued to stare at me. In slow motion, I saw his finger begin to squeeze the trigger. Then the world exploded. Billy fired his weapon. I pushed myself out of the way, but felt the shot connect with my leg. I crumpled to the floor. Schiztz. Dick fired his gun into Billy's shoulder. I didn't know if that was deliberate or a lucky shot. Either way, it felt karmic. Billy fell to the ground, screaming in agony.

Dick threw the gun to the floor and rushed to my side. I growled at him. He ignored me and instead scooped me into his arms and carried me up the cast iron steps to the cottage. He placed me on the sofa then collapsed next to me, white with effort from carrying me with his injured ankle. He closed his eyes and stroked my head absentmindedly as my blood pooled onto the cream sofa. I wanted nothing more than to sleep and let my wounds heal. Shifting when I was so injured was a bad idea, but I had a job to do first.

Chapter 15

Bracing myself for the transformation, I shifted. The roar of pain transformed into a scream as I morphed into my human form. My shoulder and leg crunched horribly as the bullets still lodged inside me ground against the bones. I should have felt lucky no major organs had been damaged but the agony was sharp. Patches cowered under the coffee table and then bolted from the room at my cries of pain. I shook with the effort. Once I'd finished the shift, I lay there panting while I got used to the pain. Dick's hand hadn't stopped stroking my head as my fur changed into my bob haircut, now decidedly messy rather than slick.

"I should call an ambulance," Dick reached for his phone.

"No ambulances," I gasped out. I fumbled for my handbag. It had materialised still looped over my uninjured shoulder as the transformation finished.

"What are you doing?"

I tilted my head to meet his eyes. They were wide with shock.

"My phone. Need to…call it in," Speaking was an effort.

"I'll get it." He eased my bag off my body and opened it up, looking inside, "Holy hellcrackers! What is this thing?"

I gave him a look. "OK, I'll find the phone first, but I want answers." I guessed he deserved them. It wasn't every day a human had a gun pointed at them, saw their landlady turn into a giant lynx and back again and shot someone. He had his arm fully into my enchanted bag as he felt for the phone. "Dzrak it!" he swore and pulled his hand out sharply. I saw a drop of blood on the end of his finger. "You got a knife in there?!"

I shrugged, then winced as the action caused a bolt of agony to course through my upper body. My vision blurred. I fought to stay awake. With a shake of his head, Dick gave up rummaging through my bag and instead leaned forward and upturned it onto the table. I watched as the contents thumped their way onto the wooden surface: my spare crossbow, a brace of bolts for it, the Fang Dagger artefact I was now using as my back up dagger, pens, tissues, an evidence bag filled with pixie dust I had forgotten to file at the Office, a spare change of underwear, my stash of cereal bars, some mints, scissors, lip gloss, a plastic baggie of catnip for personal use, and finally my phone tumbled out.

I reached out to grab it, fighting against the desire to black out. Dick felt me moving and handed it to me. He was watching my possessions continue to fall out of the bag. I left him to it and used my good hand to find the contact I was looking for.

“Do you have any idea what time it is?”

“Sorry Vass…” I panted

“What’s happened?” his voice changed from pissed off to concerned.

“Incident…my place…they saw me change.”

“Any injuries?”

“Human got shot.”

“You don’t sound so good…”

“Shotgun.”

“Silver?” At the time, it didn’t strike me as an odd thing to ask.

“No.”

There was a long pause. I guessed he was pulling up contacts on his computer. I heard a door open and shut. Was he still at the Office?

“Team will be there soon.” He hung up. Sometimes I loved that man’s efficiency. Now all I had to do was stay conscious until they got here. My eyelids flickered shut.

“Hey, hey, stay with me,” Dick’s voice pulled me back from the darkness. “What’s this do?”

I forced my eyes opened and tried to focus on the object Dick was holding. It was a poison green bottle of *Madam Mim’s Cure All*. Normally I was a big fan of the stuff but I couldn’t try to speed up my natural healing ability while there was still lead lodged inside me. I hadn’t looked at my injuries but it felt like I had daggers lodged in my limbs. "Heals people…you should try it…"

With a dubious look at the liquid, Dick took a swig, "Urgh! That's awful! You could have warned me it tasted like liquorice!"

I laughed and instantly regretted it as my body spasmed with pain. "Try rubbing it on your ankle."

I wasn't sure if the *Cure All* worked on humans but it was worth a try. Dick looked at me like I was crazy but decided to humour me. I shut my eyes.

"Hey, it does feel a little better!"

"Mmmm…" I felt the welcoming blackness fill me. I was almost gone when I heard it. The familiar sucking sound of a portal opening nearby. Vass. The team was here. I made to move, gritting my teeth against the agony.

"What are you doing? Sit back."

"Got to call them." Dick's ears hadn't caught the sound of the portal or the feet pounding through it. A shout got his attention though. He twisted on the sofa and pummelled his fist on the window, "Hey, hey, in here!"

Seconds later, the wooden door was being pushed back and the familiar body of Gwen was pushing through. She took one look at me and bellowed for a medic. A young fae ran in. I knew fae were older than they looked but she looked like a dzraking teenager. A nose ring pierced her pointed nose and an ear cuff adorned the tip of one long ear. Spiky green hair filled my vision as she ran her fingers along my injuries.

"Clothes off, we need to get that bullet out."

"Human…outside," I started weakly.

"I've got him in a holding spell. You need attention first before you heal with all that inside you. I don't want to have to open you up later to fish it out." With a flick of her hand, she vanished everything but my underwear. She was efficient, I'll give her that. I was glad I'd worn matching bra and pants today. Dick averted his eyes for modesty, but the fae immediately gave him a job.

"Hold her down. This is going to hurt."

"Shouldn't you give her some drugs or tranquilisers or something?!"

"She'll metabolise it too quickly and it might trigger her healing ability." Curse my shifter metabolism. No drugs for me. "Brace yourself, I'm going in."

I felt a light pressure as Dick pushed on my one good shoulder. Then a spark of pain exploded in the other one. Red clouds filled my vision. I forced myself to stay still, but my body had other ideas. I twitched and nearly threw Dick off the sofa.

"I said hold her!"

"I got it," Gwen strode over and heaved Dick up before taking his place. I felt her weight settle across my chest.

Another burst of pain as the fae forced something into the wound and searched for the lead shot stuck around my shoulder joint.

"Can't you use your magic?!" I glared at the young medic.

She gave me a pitying look, “It doesn’t work on lead. Too bad for you. Got to do this the old fashioned way. It might hurt a bit.”

“No schiztz!” I growled as she dug around some more. Red sparks flashed across my vision. With a snort of triumph, she pulled another piece of lead out with her tweezers and dropped it into a plastic evidence bag.

Gwen pulled a flask of something from her pocket and offered it to me. I reached out before clocking the silver colour. The harpy saw my hesitation. “It’s aluminium.”

I took a long drink of the liquid inside. It burned down my throat in a good way. I coughed before taking another slug.

“Dwarfish whisky. Strongest in the world!” she smiled. I didn’t even want to think about why she was carrying that around. Maybe we needed to have a talk when I was fully healed.

The fae had finished digging around in my shoulder and was looking for an alcohol wipe in her medical kit. She did a double take at the size of the hole and the small sealed wipe she was holding. Her bright green eyes lit on the bottle in my hand and she reached for it. I curled my hand to my chest.

“Come on, it’ll do you more good in your shoulder than your stomach.”

I disagreed with her, but conceded the bottle. I clenched my jaw as she poured it into the open wound. If looks could kill, she’d have dropped dead on the spot. As it was, she gave me a chirpy smile and moved down to my leg. Gwen smiled at me as she transferred her weight to my hips, thoughtfully tucking her dove grey wings against her back so they didn't brush me.

More pain as the medic extracted the pieces of metal one by one. It seemed like an age before they were done. Gwen stepped back, giving me some room now her strength wasn't needed to hold me down. The small fae handed me a green bottle of *Cure All* and I downed half of it.

"Want me to speed up your healing?" she waggled her fingers at me.

"Not on your life!"

She shrugged, "Have it your way." She turned to Dick and looked him up and down. "Want me to sort that ankle out for you?" I felt the sticky sweet flutter of fae magic before she flounced out of the door to deal with Billy, "You're welcome."

"How 'bout that?!" Dick was testing his weight on his healed ankle in astonishment.

Gwen ignored him, crossing her arms as she stared down at me. Her grey eyes were the same colour as storm clouds. "Right mess you've caused…again. Seems like I'm always cleaning up after you."

"Keeps you in a job," I replied weakly. I could already feel my body beginning to heal itself. I was tired but back in control. I shut my eyes.

She burst into throaty laughter and eased herself onto the floor next to me, "That it does. Keeps my life interesting too. I know you need to sleep to finish your healing but I need to ask a couple of questions first. You up for that?"

I nodded and forced my eyes back open.

"OK number one, did you bite or otherwise maim anyone?"

I shook my head.

"Next, did you shoot anyone?"

"Nope, that was all Dick."

"Huh, OK then," she turned to take in the tall man now leaning against the wall watching us. "Who saw you turn?"

"Billy, that's the one who got himself shot and his friend…and Dick here."

"Billy's out there getting some treatment now. We'll find the other one and bring them both in for questioning. Anything you want to tell me?"

I shrugged and regretted it, "They threatened a civilian. I had to act. Couldn't get to my phone to call the police or to my weapon. Things went south. No one's dead."

"Guess that'll have to do then. You want me to take him in too? Explain things to him?" she pointed with her thumb over her shoulder at Dick.

"I'm right here!"

Gwen carried on ignoring him and held my gaze. I shook my head. It was only fair that I explained things to Dick myself after what he had witnessed.

"OK then, I'll go supervise the team. Next time, call me direct. I don't want anyone else cleaning up your messes!" With a friendly squeeze of my good shoulder, she was gone. Unfurling her wings, I heard the whoosh as she took to the sky. Looking for the one who got away I guessed.

I allowed my eyes to close and drifted off into oblivion.

Chapter 16

I awoke to daylight streaming through the window. The rays hit my face and I groaned before rolling over. A dull ache pulsed in my shoulder and leg. Memories came flooding back. The storm. The gunshot. The clean-up team. I groaned again and forced myself to sit. I rolled my shoulder experimentally. The dull pain was an indication I was nearly fully healed. I allowed myself a smile in appreciation of my body's healing powers. In a few hours even the slight ache would be gone and there would be no trace of the gunshot wounds.

After I was certain I was on the road to recovery, I took in my surroundings. I was in the small double bedroom in the cottage. Light bounced off the bright walls through chinks in the curtains. I guessed it was late morning. Patches was curled up beside me, a spot of comforting warmth. I'd been out all night. I wondered where Dick had been sleeping while I'd been recovering here. It was decent of him to let me use his bed. I trailed my hand across the cotton sheets, briefly letting my mind drift to other uses of the bed. Dot was right. It had been too long.

I shook my head and got up. Patches gave a plaintive meow, stretched and padded out of the door. I followed. The pang in my leg had me limping slightly, but not too bad considering I'd been shot. I was still in my underwear since the Fae had disapparated my clothes. After a moment's hesitation, I rifled through the wooden set of drawers next to the bed. I selected a plain t-shirt and pulled it over my head. I considered finding some shorts too but Dick was tall enough that the shirt fell to my thighs. It would do. I was just shutting the drawers when the man himself walked in. His hair was tousled and wet. He smelled of moisturising soap. I guessed he'd just showered and that was why he was topless. In the bedroom. My eyes trailed down his chest and I noticed the breakfast tray laden with food. My stomach rumbled in anticipation. Healing always made me ravenous. His eyes roamed up and down my body.

"Incredible!"

I guessed he was talking about my healing wounds rather than my body. I plucked at a corner of the t-shirt before regaining my composure, "Hope you don't mind, I borrowed your shirt."

"Keep it, it looks better on you."

I gave him a shy smile. Pull it together Jones. The man has seen you in your underwear for goodness sake. "Is that for me?"

He nodded.

"You're an angel!"

He smiled, “Glad you think so. Gwen didn’t think you’d be too impressed that I moved you into the bedroom.”

I was glad I didn’t blush, “You carried me?”

A nod, “Now sit back down and have something to eat.”

I complied gladly. Breakfast in bed was a rare treat. Breakfast brought to me by a topless toned man was exceptional.

I tucked into the pile of bacon with relish. I normally preferred fruit in the morning, but my body needed to refuel after expending so much energy on fixing the large wounds.

“Better?”

I nodded as I stuffed the last of the bacon in my mouth and started on the toast.

“Do you want to tell me what happened?” his voice was low and soft. I met his chocolate brown eyes. He deserved the truth.

I finished the toast and took a sip of the coffee. He’d made it black and I ignored the small jug of milk he’d left on the tray. I nearly sighed in pleasure. It was the good beans. Then I met his gaze. “What do you want to know?”

“You turned…into an animal…how is that possible?”

“You’re the fantasy writer.” I stopped. I wasn’t being fair to him, “You know dwarves and elves exist?” He nodded along. Everyone had heard of the most populous magical races, the ones who were more integrated with mundane beings. They were tolerated with a mixture of resentment and awe for being special, for having magic. I decided to be blunt, “Well, I’m a shifter. A supernatural being. There are a few of us around…I don't have magic other than the ability to change my shape."

"Like a werewolf?"

"Yeah, except I'm a were-lynx."

He thought for a moment, "So it was you who saved me on the mountain."

"Saved is a strong word…"

"And you took a bullet for me that night. Thank you. If you hadn't been what you are, I'd be dead."

I felt that wave of heat flood my body again. I was still wary. This was the first human I'd ever told about my abilities. "So, you don't hate me?"

"Why would I hate you?" he seemed genuinely baffled.

I shrugged, "It's what happens. People find out the truth then they hunt us down, for sport. You saw those two. They wanted to kill the lion, they wanted to kill me."

"That's terrible!"

"Like I said, it's what happens."

I saw him thinking, "You said your Dad was killed…was he…?"

I took a drink of coffee, wishing it was something stronger. "Yep. He was a shifter too. He shifted in the middle of town to save a little girl from a fall. Instead of thanking him, they turned on him. Hunted him down to our house. He went outside to buy me and Mum time to leave. They tore him apart right in front of our house. It takes a lot to kill us without the right, uh, tools, but…they managed it. Mum took us as far away from that town as she could. Moved us out to rural Wales. Kept us apart, or as apart as she could given I insisted on going to the local school…I don't like to think about it."

"I'm sorry that happened to you…and no…I don't hate you." The look he gave me was full of concern, and something else.

"I don't want your pity," I shook myself, "What other questions have you got?"

He stared at me for a second, "OK…is it true about the full moon?"

"Unfortunately, yes. It triggers something in our brains, forces a change."

"How does that work?" I furrowed my brow in confusion. "I mean, you living out here, I get it. Lots of wide open spaces, as long as no one's trying to hunt you. But you said you've lived in London, how can you change then without anyone noticing?"

"Most big cities have agreed full moon roaming rights in their larger parks and it's not like we lose ourselves completely. The human side is still there, it just takes more effort to control the…other side. We act more like animals, so a good run in the park, some fights with other shifters, it helps keep the animal at bay the rest of the month."

He thought that over, then asked another question, "Does it hurt, when you…change?"

"Yeah, it's not a pleasant experience but, you get used to it. Besides there are some benefits to being a shifter."

"Like you're ability to heal."

I raised my coffee mug in a toast, "It comes in handy."

"And the medic was…"

"A fae."

He nodded, still thinking, "And Gwen?…I've been too scared to ask what she is!"

I laughed, she had that effect on people, "She's a harpy, just be grateful she wasn't in her full bird form. Wait, she's still here?"

"Yep, she insisted on staying, we've been working on the house while you were out for the count."

"What? You've been working on the house since last night?!"

He gave me a look, "You've been out for three days! I was worried, but Gwen said you'd be fine."

"Three days! Dzrak! That's the longest I've been out for." I stared off into middle distance contemplating the events of that night. It must have been bad.

"One more question…" there was something about the way he said it that pulled me back from my introspection and made my stomach do a little flip. I caught his eyes and raised my eyebrow. He leaned in and tucked a strand of hair behind my ear tenderly "…now you're all better, can I do what I've been wanting to do since the car?"

"What's that?" my voice came out breathy, a hoarse whisper.

"Kiss you."

I put down my mug on the bedside table and leaned into him. Our lips connected. It started soft then his hands were splayed through my hair. I responded and wrapped my arms around his neck, pulling him closer.

Gwen burst into the room, "I thought I heard you, this came for you…oh!" She crossed her arms as we pulled apart, the padded envelope she was holding rumpled. "No, no, you carry on, don't mind me!"

The breakfast tray tumbled to the floor with a crash. Dick sprang up and began picking up the plates. With a wicked grin, the harpy walked out, "Meet me at the house when you're done!"

I groaned and got out the other side of the bed. Great. Now I was going to be the subject of her merciless teasing. I snuck a glance at the tall man mopping the floor with a napkin. Maybe it was worth it. Dick caught me looking and gave me a wink before taking the tray and the debris back to the kitchen. I followed him out, limping slightly. I refilled my coffee cup and made one for Dick before I opened the envelope. A small black box fell out. It looked like a Dictaphone. I picked up the note.

This might be useful. Keep it in your handbag, Maxi.

Strange. I tested it out by saying hello a few times. I replayed it and was nearly deafened by my own voice. I shook my head in irritation. Dick swore. Maxi could never resist meddling with technology. I packed it away in my bag. I started to walk over to the main house. Dick offered me his arm but I waved him away, I could still walk dammit.

The house was surrounded by scaffolding but underneath, I could see subtle changes. The shutters were all rehung on the front and had been repainted in a deep blue colour that accented the stonework on the house.

"Gwen's been a big help," Dick was rambling. I let him fill the silence, "she can fly so she's been helping Sam on the roof and she rehung those top shutters with no problems at all."

I looked up, the harpy was indeed on the roof. She was using her hands to take off the slate tiles and placing them into a heavy duty bag hung from the chimney. When it was full, she unhooked the bag, flew down and lined them all up in a neat row, sorting any broken ones from those that could be reused. It was an unorthodox building method but it worked. They were already half way done with stripping the roof.

"Nice work, I think you missed your calling!" I called over. She turned and gave me a look.

"I wish I'd missed your make out session this morning, no one needs to see that!" I groaned and she slapped me on the back, "Hey, just kidding, it's good to see you with someone, I just don't need to see what you do with them!"

I closed my eyes and forced myself to count to ten. I heard a rattling sound. When I looked, Sam was making his way down a ladder, followed by another builder I guessed was his partner.

“Glad to see you’re awake! That was some flu you had.” I looked at Gwen, who shrugged. Really helpful. “Gwen’s been brilliant though, I didn’t know you knew any supernaturals. We don’t get them much round here, but my Claire’s a big fan.” I smiled my thanks at his accepting the tall winged woman in front of him.

“I’ve been trying to recruit this one as my partner instead of Sam, but she’s insisting on going back to her day job.” The other builder joked. He gave her a dig in the ribs with his elbow.

My eyes widened, I don’t think I’d seen Gwen let anyone touch her without her permission, at least not without causing them some serious pain.

Gwen gave me a wink, “I’m gone at the end of the day.”

The builder’s face fell, “Not straight away…” he said hopefully.

The harpy sized him up. “We’ll see.”

I raised my eyebrows at her. She was one to talk. If my instincts were anything to go by, she was already sleeping with my builder. The men started inside and I hung back to talk to Gwen, “Sleeping with him huh? And you’re giving me grief!”

“Well we’re not doing much sleeping…” she gave me a wink coupled with a smile and turned to follow them inside. I shook my head and followed. She was incorrigible.

They stuck me on so-called light cleaning duties while I was recovering, because I insisted on doing something. I dusted, swept and mopped, building up a sweat. They checked on me regularly throughout the day, trying to be casual about it. Gwen brought me a cup of strong coffee. Dick made sure I stopped for lunch. Sam came down from the roof to talk me through his plans for the house, forcing me to take a break from the endless cleaning. Even his assistant was sent in with a slice of cake mid-afternoon. I was getting sick of all the care taking and was glad when they all called it quits at four o' clock. Gwen gave me a wink as she slid into the builders' van. I shook my head at her in mock despair.

That left me and Dick alone on the farm.

"Fancy a ride?"

I spluttered on my cup of coffee, nearly choking on my drink. Then I saw his thumb pointing over his shoulder to his bike. I wiped myself down with as much dignity as I could muster and nodded.

He let me wear his leather jacket for protection and I dug out a helmet from the barn. It was for my quad bike rather than a full visor biker helmet but it would do.

I tucked myself snugly against his body as he drove. The wind blew dust and bugs into my face as we picked up speed. I closed my eyes and leaned my face into his back for protection. It was exhilarating being blind and trusting someone else to lead the way for a change. I surrendered control. We crested the mountain and he pulled to a stop in a dusty layby. I felt him put down the kick stand and turn off the engine. I pulled myself from my tight grip around his waist and climbed off the bike.

I took off my helmet and rested it on the seat, before I stepped from the layby and walked the short distance to a low fence. It was the edge of a steep drop down a face of sheer rock. I caught a mountain goat picking its way along the cliff face. Dick came up behind me and looped his arms loosely around me.

"I never get tired of the views round here," I sighed and leaned back against his chest.

"Beautiful," he whispered against my ear. Goosebumps trickled along my neck at his breath.

Then my back pocket started beeping and vibrating violently.

Great. All the messages I'd missed being out of signal were catching up with me now. I reached back to grab my phone.

"Sorry, let me just turn it off." I frowned at the device in my hand as the noise continued. How many messages did I miss? I scrolled through my home screen and saw twenty missed calls and many texts and emails. I checked who the calls were from. Dot and Maxi. The last call was from Maxi earlier today. I didn't like this at all.

Chapter 17

I shrugged Dick away and asked him to give me a minute while I checked these messages. He didn't look happy about it but when he saw how worried I looked, he said he was going to admire the scenery. I scrolled through the texts. Mostly voicemail notifications, but there were a couple from my team mates:

Call me when you get this. Dot

Maxi here. Found something important boss.

I need to talk to you. Dot

Sent you the files boss.

I'm going in tonight boss.

Maxi's in trouble. Dot

My frown deepened and I dialled my voicemail. It started with Maxi's excited voice, "Boss, I found something très excitant. I've sent you a picture, call me back, what should I do?"

I sifted through the mostly worried messages from Dot:

"Have you seen the picture? Call me."

"Have you heard what Maxi's doing? Call me."

"I know you and he are going through a bad patch, but you should call him, he's getting worked up. Call me."

They went on. There was one from a spam insurance company too asking if I'd been in an accident lately. I deleted it.

I scrolled back through my messages until I found the pictures Maxi had sent. They were of an itinerary. I zoomed in. The Director's itinerary. I scrolled down, trying to see what had got Maxi so excited. It took me a few tries but I found it. Every month on the second Saturday, the Director had a private appointment at midnight. That was suspicious. It was at the same London club each time. Pendragon. I'd never heard of the name of it, so I searched it on the internet. It looked like a typical gentleman's club on the outside. Brass panels, painted red door, fancy footman outside in a red uniform. The pictures inside showed leather armchairs and smoking rooms. In fact it looked so archetypal, I frowned at it. Did these places even exist any more?

I checked the date on my phone. Today was the second Saturday of the month. According to the appointment time, the meeting was starting tonight at midnight.

I dialled Maxi's number. No answer. I typed out a quick message for him to call me then called Dot.

“Finally! Where have you been?!” the vampire sounded annoyed. I didn’t blame her.

“Sorry, the signal’s lousy here.”

“I didn’t realise you were stuck in the eighteenth century!”

“OK, I’m here now. What’s occurring?”

“Maxi’s been in touch. He was panicking when he couldn’t get through to you but now he reckons he’s got something big. He’s saying he thinks it’s bigger than the Director and he’s got a chance to redeem himself.”

“What does that mean?”

“It means he feels awful for what happened and he wants to get back in your good books. I think he’s going to do something stupid.”

I thought back to the text messages, “I think you’re right. Any idea what he’s going to do?”

“He’s talking about breaking into some club. He excited, he’s sorting some tech out.”

“Who’s he taking in with him?”

“No one, he wants to do it by himself. Believe me, I’ve offered, but he won’t listen.”

I swore, “Dzrak it! Why’s he going on a field op by himself?!”

“Do you want me to go after him?”

I pinched the bridge of my nose while I thought through a plan. Just then I got a call holding noise in my ear. I checked my phone's display.

"Maxi's calling, hang on!"

I switched calls with the press of a button, "Maxi! Thank goodness! Are you alright?"

"I'm fine, really good, yah, peachy" his voice sounded shaky, "I've found it Jones, this is where it's all happening."

"Where what's all happening?"

"You saw the pictures?"

"And? There's a meeting tonight at some London club."

"Yah, I spoke to some friends of mine who know all the best clubs in the city and they haven't heard of this place. It's shady. I'm sure. I'm going to go tonight and find out what's going on."

"Right, I'm glad you've found something, but Maxi, don't take this the wrong way…your skills are more tech than breaking and entering."

"Oh I'm not breaking and entering, I'm going to walk in."

"What?!" I exploded down the phone, "Don't even think about it. I'm coming to see you, we'll think up a plan together."

"Er, Jones, don't take this the wrong way but I'm far more likely to get into a gentleman's club than you are." He was right, he probably knew all the secret handshakes thanks to his time at a posh boarding school. "Vass is going to get me an introduction anyway."

"Vass?" Something felt off.

"Said he knew someone. Anyway, don't worry, I've rigged up a camera, you can watch me via live stream if you want."

"Of course I want! Send me that link immediately and don't do anything until I get there! We'll think up a plan that doesn't involve you putting yourself in danger."

He hung up. I stared at the phone. Great. An insistent beeping told me that Dot was still holding the line. I jabbed my screen.

"I'm back."

"And?"

"Maxi's going to infiltrate some shady gentleman's club that's somehow involved with supernaturals."

Dot gave a low whistle.

"I'm going to London." I made my decision.

"Do you want me to meet you there?"

"No, best not. No one's tracking my movement as far as I know but if they call the Office and no one's there…too risky."

"I don't like it."

"Neither do I but look, you can cover for us and handle any calls that come in."

“O..K..”

“I mean it Dot! Stay in Cardiff!”

She hung up. I had a bad feeling about this.

Chapter 18

A ping on my phone told me that Maxi had sent through the link to the live stream. I clicked it and a small grey circle rotated around the screen. Great. I couldn't figure out if it was connection issues or if Maxi just hadn't started it yet. I swore at my phone and hit the refresh button several times in a row, tapping my foot as I got more frustrated.

"Everything alright, chief?" Dick interrupted my frantic refreshing just as I was considering throwing the phone over the edge of the mountain. Instead I forced myself to take a deep breath. I explained the situation to Dick. I decided to come clean about my job and the reason I was on sabbatical. I didn't know what was going to happen between us, but he'd already seen me shift so I figured I might as well be completely honest. His expression turned from disbelief to concern as I raced through the story in short sentences.

"So, basically, I need to grab some things and head to London tonight to stop my friend from doing something stupid."

"OK," he thought a moment, "I'm coming too."

I shook my head, "You're a civilian. I'm not risking any more lives. I don't even know what the situation is."

"I don't want to get involved in your…operation…but you can't drive and monitor a live stream. Let me drive you there. I'll find a hotel, stay out of your way. You can find me when it's over."

"You mean that? You'll stay out of the way, you won't try to be a hero?"

"Scout's honour," he made a salute and then gave a slight bow as he motioned for me to mount the bike, "Your chariot awaits."

I tried to stop from smiling as I climbed on. He gave one of my hands a reassuring squeeze, "It's going to be alright."

"I hope so," I muttered in reply.

We got back to the house in record time and I threw things into my enchanted crocodile skin handbag haphazardly.

"You want the kitchen sink too?!" Dick asked as I picked up the Fang Dagger and placed it in the bag, followed by a box of matches.

"I want to be prepared," I retorted as I added a selection of sharp kitchen knives. He shook his head, bemused as he tossed a spare change of clothes into his backpack and walked to the car. I sprinted over to the barn for a blowtorch. Fire was always useful against magical beings. I put it carefully into my bag. I considered trying to muscle one of the ladders currently on the side of my house in, but decided there were limits and instead selected a coil of rope from on top of some dusty boxes.

I stuck the bag in the back of my standard issue grey Volvo and then thought for a second. If we were going to a fancy London club, I might need a smarter outfit than my current jeans and t-shirt. I ran back inside and grabbed one of my tailored suits and a pair of stiletto shoes. At least I'd brought something smart with me, and I felt more confident in my work gear. I slung the suit and shoes into the car and clambered into the passenger seat. Dick had settled himself into the driver's seat and was readjusting the mirrors. It felt odd not driving myself. I liked to be in control.

"Right, let's go," I forced myself to do up my seatbelt and not insist we swap.

Dick nodded and turned the car round before heading along the bumpy track to the main road. He stalled once. "Damn stick shift!"

I shook my head and tried to suppress a smile, "You sure you can handle this thing?"

He smiled back, "I've handled things a lot more powerful than this, little lady." I hit him lightly on the arm for that remark. He laughed good naturedly. It lightened the mood, helped me forget why we were setting off on this road trip, helped me put the fact that my friend and colleague was in danger.

"Me and Sally just need to get to know each other." He drew my thoughts away from Maxi. I watched as he ran his hand over the steering wheel lightly to emphasise his point.

"You named my car?! What is it with people naming vehicles?"

"Helps the vehicles to respond," he looked serious.

"OK, why Sally?"

"She just looked like a Sally…and, uh, the registration starts with SL and has a Y in it."

I rolled my eyes as he pulled onto the main road. My phone pinged. Finally the live stream was up. Maxi's face filled my screen in extreme close up. I jolted backwards in surprise.

"Testing, testing, one two three. Feed is now live!" he stepped back and I recognised the plain white tiles and black walls from the Magical Liaison Office's London branch. I realised he was looking in the mirror and holding up his own phone to test the stream.

"No schiztz," I muttered. "How do I talk to you?" I asked the screen.

I knew he couldn't hear me but he answered anyway, "I've sent you an audio link. It's a secure channel. Talk into your phone once you click it and I'll be able to hear you. You should hear me through the other feed. I'll give you two minutes to respond, yah?"

I watched him send me a link on his phone. It popped up on my screen and I clicked it. Nothing seemed to happen. I tried talking into my phone, "Maxi?"

“Loud and clear! Repeat I can hear you loud and clear!”

“Calm down Maxi!”

“Right, right, sorry. Got a bit carried away!”

“Why are you wearing those glasses?”

“I thought the camera should go in them, good idea what!”

I groaned, “But you don’t wear glasses!” I didn’t bother to point out that they were massive frames that looked incredibly suspicious.

“They don’t know that!”

“Vass does!”

“Ah, right, well, I thought they won’t make me take off glasses but they might search my jacket, you know if they’re onto me. Anyway, this is my decoy!” He took a massive pin badge with his school logo on it and attached it to his blazer jacket. He was right. The logo of a pig’s head being carried by a lion was so awful, no one would notice the glasses.

“Was that really your school’s logo?”

“Well, my house in the school. Leones domin-ah-te!” he quoted in Latin, then for my benefit, “Lions rule! Our arch rivals were the boars, bloody porkys! Beat them in cricket every year!”

“Right, what’s the plan?” I pulled him back from reliving his glory days.

“I’m going to check out the building, see if there’s a back way in. If not, I’ll go in the front.”

It was a terrible plan. "You can go scope the building but wait until I'm there before you try to go in. Understood?"

He stared sullenly at the mirror.

"Understood?" I put more force into my voice.

"Yah, yah. Over and out."

I didn't bother to point out that it wasn't a walkie talkie. He walked away from the mirror and soon I could see the corridors of the Office. He seemed to be looking away from people and he quickly left the building and headed into a nearby tube station. I propped the phone up on the dashboard, opened the window and cranked up the volume on the radio. It was set to a station that played the best of the nineties.

"Uh, you mind turning that down?" Maxi's voice hissed through my phone. Oops. I frantically grabbed the phone away from the speaker and whispered sorry. Maxi grumbled to himself. I hit the mute button on my phone and kept the volume on the car radio down as we carried on driving. Dick was not looking impressed. I pressed my lips together and stared out of the window. It was a gorgeous day. I would have enjoyed the drive if I wasn't embarrassed at my ineptitude at using technology, racing to do surveillance on my Director and stop my friend from doing something stupid.

The drive felt interminable. We hit traffic a few times as we jostled with holiday makers clogging up the motorways. The sat nav app changed routes so many times, Dick was in a constant fight with the robotic voice.

"Turn left."

"You want me to go where?"

"She said turn left…there!"

"Now stay on the road for ten miles."

"Ten miles on this tiny track?!"

"That's what she said…"

"Son of a gun, is that a tractor heading for us?!"

"Just pull in at the layby by there!"

He hyperventilated as the farmer gave us a wave and trundled past.

"Right, do you want me to drive?"

"No, no, it's OK. I'm just not used to these roads any more. Let me get my bearings. In the US everything was wider! It would help if the sat nav wasn't taking us to the bum end of nowhere!"

I let him vent at the sat nav and glanced at the live stream. Maxi was still making his way across London. The sounds of the city filtered through my phone. It was a stark contrast to the peacefulness of the country that I had been beginning to enjoy again. Sirens blared, the drunks on the cramped underground tube stations ranted, city workers talked about their day and their evening plans. It almost made me nostalgic for my time in London. Almost.

Maxi had initially been giving me a running commentary of his movements and expected arrival time. I had unmuted my phone and hissed at him to stop, but he was still sounding suspicious as he announced every single tube stop. Through the camera, I saw a few people give him odd looks, but compared to some of the other travellers, he was relatively normal. I shook my head and rolled my eyes even though he couldn't see my reaction. Eventually he found the club. The stream showed a non-descript London building, flanked on one side by a high-priced hipster coffee shop advertising infused foam toppers and on the other side by a tailor's shop with smartly dressed mannequins in the window. It didn't look suspicious to me. Maxi walked past it three times, going up and down the street. I caught a glimpse of his reflection in a shop window. He had clearly run his hands through his already wild hair a number of times, making it stick up like a crazy professor. Combined with his large glasses, he only needed a lab coat to look as if he might be some sort of Back to the Future cosplayer. He was acting what he thought was nonchalantly. Obviously this meant he was sticking out like a sore thumb. I turned off the car radio and spoke into the phone.

"Stop just walking up and down the street! Stop looking around at everything like you're trying to spot something. Go in somewhere, look at a shop."

"Roger that!"

"And stop talking to me!"

"Which way is that machine trying to take us now?!" Dick cut across our covert conversation.

I glanced at the map on Dick's phone, "Right at the end of this lane."

"Who's that?"

"I said stop talking to me! It's Dick, he's my…lodger. He offered to drive so I could keep you under surveillance."

"He sounds nice, say hi from me!"

"Hi Maxi!"

"Stop having a conversation!" I glared at Dick then spoke into the phone, "Go into a shop."

Maxi mumbled something then opened the closest shop door and went in. The door had a blacked out panel. I had a bad feeling about this. As the camera's stream shifted to adjust to the neon lighting inside, I caught brightly coloured feather boas and a lot of black. The camera turned in a slow circle as Maxi took it in. The rack of magazines with x-rated titles. A display of adult toys in bright colours. A disinterested young woman with piercings all over her face stood at a low counter, flipping the pages of a magazine. I caught sight of Maxi's face in a mirrored surface. His eyes were wide like a baby deer caught in the headlights.

"Can I help you?" the woman didn't even look up from her magazine.

"What? I mean yah, yah, I'll take er…this," he grabbed the nearest thing off the display and rushed to the counter. I saw him put a box of edible underwear on the pristine countertop. The lady bagged it in a paper bag and took his money, "Yah, thanks."

"Just turn around and get out Maxi," I made my voice soft and calm, like I was talking to a frightened animal, which I was.

He followed my instructions, his hands trembling as he opened the door. Outside, he leant against the wall and I could hear him breathing deeply. The paper bag rustled in his hands. So this club wasn't in as nice a part of London as I'd thought.

"You did great, now how about a drink. Did I see a pub across from the club?"

Maxi scanned the street and went into the pub. He ordered a pint of cider and picked a table near the window where he could compose himself and watch the club. About halfway down the pint, he mumbled, "Did you see that place?"

"I did, you did great."

"There were…"

"Best not to dwell on it," I wondered how naïve he could be, after all he had gone to a private boarding school.

I watched as he pushed the paper bag to one side and carried on drinking. A couple of middle aged men in suits entered the club. They looked like wealthy city types wanting a drink. Maxi's stream clicked as he took pictures of them. A few seconds later, their names appeared on my stream. I was impressed. Maxi had managed to link face recognition to his prototype spy camera and had accessed the Driver and Vehicle Licensing Authority and crime databases. A speeding ticket flashed up and a parking fine. Minor misdemeanours. Both men came out again after about an hour. There was nothing I could see that flagged them as supernaturals or a threat.

After his nerves had settled, Maxi decided to go for another walk.

"You forgot your package!" A helpful bartender called after him. Maxi's reflection in a faded pub mirror blushed beetroot red as he mumbled his thanks and grabbed the crumpled paper bag.

Clutching it tightly, he tried to circle around the back of the building. It was tucked behind a brick wall with a solid looking gate on it. Maxi gave it a tentative push then leaned against it as a delivery bike pedalled past.

"Top of the afternoon to you sah!" The delivery driver nearly fell off his bike as he turned to give Maxi a confused look.

"No one says that Maxi!" He was not doing a good job of staying discreet. No one acknowledged anyone else in London. It was how the city dwellers got by without thinking of their fellow citizens. After all, if you started talking to people on the street, the next place would be on the tube. I shuddered as I imagined having to strike up a conversation with strangers in those cramped compartments.

Maxi crossed the road and took a long look at the part of the building that stretched above the wall. It was tall, but not a skyscraper. The brickwork was less fancy at the back and an ancient fire escape crisscrossed down past the blacked out windows. I didn't like the look of the blacked out windows, but it was always useful to know where the escape routes were.

"That's all you can do for now, go back and have another drink. See who comes and goes. I'll be there soon enough."

"Roger that."

"Over and out Maxi," I huffed out a sigh. This was going to be the least undercover surveillance operation in history.

Before we joined the motorway, I decided to change into my suit. There was less traffic here and fewer police cars or traffic cameras. I didn't fancy flashing anyone as I got dressed. I climbed inelegantly into the back seat and began stripping. Dick's eyes caught mine in the mirror. I lifted my eyebrows and he looked away. I smiled. It was nice to confirm he was still interested. Perhaps after all this was over, we could finally enjoy some alone time in a nice London hotel. I got changed in record time despite the cramped conditions. I left the jacket hanging from the handle above the door and clambered back into the front seat, my spiked stiletto heels in hand. I slipped them on and settled back into my seat, strapping myself back in.

The sun had set by the time we entered the outskirts of London. After some finagling on the phone to pay the congestion charge, I played through the options for getting into the club and seeing what the Director was up to at midnight. Most of them involved violence.

Three half pints and a packet of crisps in, Maxi was getting restless. I saw his hands tapping on the table and his constant glances at the club's entrance.

We were getting close to the street but stuck in city traffic when two figures appeared walking side by side on the brightly lit street. Even under the artificial lighting, I recognised my boss. Vass. The other figure was taller, leaner. The Director? I couldn't quite make out his face under a pinstriped trilby hat.

Maxi had spotted them too. He stood up and downed the remaining liquid in his glass. "I'm going in!"

“Maxi no! Wait for me!” he ignored me and kept going. “Maxi, if you don’t stop this instant I’ll, I’ll…I’ll give you a bad performance report.”

I watched him stiffen slightly. He craved positive performance reports. I wouldn’t be surprised if he framed each evaluation he received alongside his many academic qualifications. But he kept going. I started to open the car door, intent on racing across the remaining streets and stopping him. Dick pulled me back.

“Don’t blow it for him, have a little faith. We’ll be there soon.”

I took my hand off the handle. Dick was right. The team trusted me, I had to trust my team. And I did trust Maxi, I realised, even if he was an eager fool. I held my breath as he walked straight past the discreet brass plaque that held the name of the club and pushed open the heavy doors.

The door opened onto a small reception area. It looked old and expensive with wood panelling and leather seats. Vass and the other man turned as he entered behind them. Even in the faded fake candlelight, I could see it was the Director. Dzrak. I felt myself tense as they recognised Maxi. Then Vass smiled and leaned over to the uniformed man standing at the tall reception desk.

The man asked Maxi for his name and gestured for him to sign in. I watched his neat signature spell out Maximillian Baskerville in black ink on a thick page. Then he followed Vass and the Director through a pair of wooden doors into the club. I expected them to stop at the well-stocked bar, manned by a waiter in a neat waistcoat over a crisp white shirt or sit on one of the well-used leather sofas. Instead, they walked to a brass lift and pressed a button. I couldn’t tell if they were going up or down. The lift shuddered to a halt and the lights flickered.

Vass turned to Maxi and looked directly into the camera, "You won't be needing these." I watched helplessly as he pulled them from Maxi's face and heard a crunch as he snapped them in half. The feed went dead.

Chapter 19

"Dzrak it!" We were still too far away for me to usefully do anything. I tapped my foot impatiently. A message from Dot popped up. I called her immediately.

"What is it?"

"Not good. I had my contacts do some digging on that club. It's a hotspot for some nefarious supernaturals as well as serious city hotshots." She reeled off the names. I recognised at least one from the Magical Liaison Office's watchlist, a politician and the head of a big tech firm.

"And you didn't find this out before?!"

"Sorry boss."

I hung up. Now I was even more worried about Maxi. I spent the time pulling weapons out of my handbag. The Fang Dagger went in my belt. I strapped my crossbow holster to my thigh and made sure my bow was loaded before putting it in. I rearranged the knives and bolts in my bag so they were more easily accessible. Then I sat there, tense and frustrated, ready to run for it as soon as we were close.

"Hey, it'll be alright."

I stared at Dick, "You don't know that. Just stay clear. I'll meet you at the hotel if I survive."

He paled. I was asking a lot of him to accept this world and my job as well as my shifter nature. He pulled up at the end of the street. I opened the door then leaned in and gave him a hard kiss on the lips. I'd made my decision. If I made it out, I wanted Dick.

I stalked down the street. It was after dark and quiet. I didn't like it. Surely even the more out of the way parts of London were busy at night. The gloomy pub light illuminated the road. Further down I saw the neon sign above the sex shop Maxi had entered earlier. I took a deep breath outside the heavy club doors then pushed them open.

The scent of pine wood polish mingled with leather made me wrinkle my nose as I stepped inside. The young man on reception looked me up and down, and raised an eyebrow in a question. I stayed silent and stared him down. He broke our staring contest after two seconds and coughed nervously.

"Can I help you?"

"I'm here for Vass."

"I'm afraid this is a gentleman's only club…"

"And?"

"You're not..." he trailed off.

I tried a knowing smile, "I'm, er, an exception...the, er, entertainment."

He frowned as he took in my smart suit, high heels and the crossbow strapped to my thigh.

"I wasn't aware anyone had ordered any...entertainment. But I'm afraid ladies are only permitted to enter the club on Tuesday lunchtimes or the last Sunday of every month. Club rules."

I moved closer and stepped around his desk in one sharp movement. His hand reached for a phone. I grabbed his arm, preventing him from moving. I pressed against him and whispered, "Right, there are two ways this can go..." My free hand hovered above the holster on my thigh. His eyes widened as he focused on the sharp bolt in the crossbow. He swallowed twice.

"OK, OK, you can go in."

"Excellent. Now tell me where Vass has gone."

"I need to check the log."

"Of course," I ripped the phone off the desk, severing the cables before releasing his arm. I stayed close, breathing down his neck as he frantically flicked through a leather diary where they kept booking details.

"He's, uh, in the, uh, basement room. It's a private party. You can't go down there!"

My gaze caught on Maxi's signature printed in an open log book. Looks like he was the only non-member in tonight. I stabbed the Fang Dagger into the bright red panic alarm under the desk. Sparks glittered around the blade.

I smiled ferociously and the man backed away against the wall, "Like I said, I'm the entertainment."

I left him cowering behind his desk and strolled into the bar. The tang of leather was stronger here, mixed with whisky and old wood. The bartender looked up and gave a start at seeing a woman in the club. He frowned then his eyes widened as he focused on something behind me. I whirled round, dagger in hand. Dot grinned at me and raised her hands in mock surrender. I breathed out a sigh.

"I thought I told you to stay in Cardiff."

"Like I was going to let you have all the fun."

I nodded, "Alright, make sure no one does anything stupid." The vampire nodded and smiled at the staff who were now gaping at us.

I walked past a club member sleeping underneath a newspaper and two others playing cards. They didn't even look up as I walked to the lift. I pushed a brass button then stepped in when the doors slid open. I pressed the polished button with a 'B' for basement and unholstered my crossbow. The weight felt good in my hands. The lift slowed and the doors opened onto a hallway lit with electric flickering candles. Atmospheric. I sniffed and stepped out. Spicy aftershave mixed with newspapers and the sparky scent of burnt electronics told me that Maxi had gone this way. No blood. He was alive. Or had been drained by a vampire. I forced my thoughts away from that possibility.

I followed the hallway. At each door, I paused and allowed my nose to lead the way. There was a cleaning closet, an empty office and finally a room filled with people. Magical beings. Their scents were too strong and too varied, mingling into each other. I listened carefully, trying to get a feel for how many people were inside. I weighed up my options. I was normally all for the direct approach, but Maxi could be in danger. Silently, I headed back down the hall.

I tried the door of the cleaning cupboard. It was unlocked. Who would want to steal cleaning supplies? There was a metal trolley. I loaded it up with sprays and cloths. A broom and a mop were already neatly attached to one end. Perfect. I dug around in my handbag until I found a roll of duct tape. I attached one of my spare knives to the mop head. As I reversed the trolley out, I saw an overcoat hanging from a peg in the same green as the uniform waistcoats upstairs. I slipped it on over my suit jacket.

I used my bum to push open the sleek double doors and bustled in with the trolley. The low murmur of voices stopped instantly. I kept my head down and moved quickly to a corner of the room. The wheels clattered as I went. Not exactly a subtle entrance. I counted out of the corner of my eye. Twelve. Plus Maxi. Still alive and sitting at the table. He was sweating and looking around. One of the men coughed loudly. I ignored him and flicked a duster at a light.

"We are still meeting in here," one of them bristled, astonished that a cleaner would dare to enter an occupied room. I tensed.

“Now, now, that’s no way to treat our guest,” I recognised the Director’s voice. I tensed. “Won’t you have a seat Agent Jones?”

I felt the compulsion ooze from him. I resisted. Instead, I turned slowly, slipping my crossbow from under a pile of cloths on the table.

“How about you tell me what’s going on?”

He laughed at that. A high-pitched sound. It grated on my ears. I ground my teeth together and kept my crossbow aimed at him. He gave a small nod. Two males in suits stood and walked confidently towards me. One troll, one elf. I adjusted my aim. The first bolt hit the elf in the knee. He fell to the ground with a scream. I reloaded at supernatural speed. I turned and hit the troll in the shoulder. He grunted with pain and kept coming. I dropped the crossbow onto the trolley and yanked the mop from its clip. The troll laughed, and gestured to his friends at the table. A couple of them guffawed too. A couple more looked nervous. He pushed his long greasy hair over his shoulder and raised his fists in a martial arts stance.

I jabbed the mop handle at his face. He raised his guard. I spun the mop around and hit him in the stomach. Hard. His mouth dropped open as the knife I’d attached to it sunk into his flesh. I yanked the mop out and blood poured onto the floor. The muddy metallic smell of troll blood filled my nostrils.

“Get her!” the Director yelled.

A werewolf transformed in front of me and pounced. I sidestepped his leap and picked up my blowtorch from the trolley. I flicked the switch but it didn’t light. I tried again. I looked at the blowtorch and at the wolf, which had turned and was now sporting an animal grin on its furry face. I threw the useless blowtorch at its face and retrieved my Fang Dagger from the trolley. He prowled towards me. We squared off in front of each other. I tossed the knife from hand to hand as I looked for an opening. The wolf's mouth opened. Saliva dripped onto the floor. His paws moved impatiently. He leapt again. I ran to the other corner of the room, jumped and shifted into my lynx form. He followed. I used the wall to give me height and landed on his back. I dug my claws in hard, raking through his furry hide. He howled and bucked as he tried to shake my grip. With another leap, I was gone. His wounds were already closing. He turned to face me. His yellow eyes met my amber ones. He charged and leapt. I ran forward and ducked. Underneath him, I transformed back to my human form, twisted and rammed the dagger into his stomach up to its jewelled hilt. His momentum took him forward. The knife ripped his underbelly open. I held onto the handle. Guts spilled onto the carpeted floor. I winced at the carpet burns on my back as I skidded away from him. He was panting still but he was out of the fight.

Another troll stood and towered over me. I rolled between his legs, aiming a kick at his groin. I heard his sharp intake of breath as I connected. He doubled over. He turned to me, tears leaking down his face. I shoved a swivel chair on wheels at him and sprinted back to the trolley. I needed more weapons. He grabbed the back of the overall coat I was wearing. I felt myself pulled backwards. I turned deftly, spinning my arms out of the garment. He was left holding the coat. He dropped it with a roar and pushed the chair aside. I made it to the cart and grabbed another knife.

I threw it in his direction. The force of my throw sunk it deep into his eye. He fell to the ground with a scream.

I backed into the injured elf as I scanned the room for the next attack. His eyes were wide and his mouth was opening and closing as he took in the scene. He limped away from me as quickly as he could, back to his seat "I've had enough of this!" He pressed a metallic box on the table. The sucking sound of a portal forming filled my ears. A glowing oval appeared above the box. I swore softly. So this was what the portal research the Office had paid for had created. It looked like it had been successful. The elf dragged himself onto the table, grabbed the box and stumbled through. The portal closed behind him.

I adjusted my grip on my dagger and stood in a wide stance. The other figures exchanged glances then reached for their own portal devices on the table. I reloaded my crossbow. Too late. The portals were already open and the figures were diving through the oval gates. I fired after one of them. The bolt thudded into the wall as the portal closed.

I turned. Vass and the Director were still there. They were standing now, with Maxi between them. He looked pale.

"It's alright Maxi."

"Oh, that's priceless! She still thinks you're working for her!"

I looked between the three of them. What the dzrak was going on?

"Let him go and I won't hurt you!"

"I don't think you've got any leverage here. Why don't you go and disarm her Maxi?" Vass turned to my friend and gave a nasty smile before turning back to me, "Don't blame him, he's smart enough to know the only way is to join us. It's a shame you had to get so involved, if only you had stayed in Wales..."

I tried to process the betrayal here as Maxi apologetically removed my crossbow and dagger. He placed them on the large table in the centre of the room. I eyed them. Not too far away. Plus I had a knife strapped to my ankle. He hadn't patted me down…

"Now on your knees and hands behind your head," Vass had pulled his own crossbow from somewhere and was calmly aiming it at me. "You could have just taken the sabbatical and left well enough alone you know, or you could have died when you got shot, but no. Not the intrepid Agent Jones. You were a good agent though, I'd have asked you to join us if you weren't so straight and narrow."

I thought back through my conversations with Vass. "You wanted me out of the picture, back at home. You encouraged me to go!" I thought some more, "You weren't asking if I was OK when you asked if they had silver in their guns. You set me up!"

Vass gave a slow clap, "Well done. You finally caught up. If those idiots could just have followed my orders..."

"But you sent out a team…"

"Yes, if the harpy hadn't walked in while I was taking your call, this would all have been taken care of already."

So that was it. He'd paid some locals to harass me, maybe even kill me, and counted on there being no response. My eyes narrowed. I knew my pupils were turning into slits.

“Now, now, don’t do anything stupid Jones. I think you know how this is going to go. We’re going to kill you and then take over the world!” he monologued like a dzraking villain in a comic book. I could have laughed if I wasn’t about to die.

“You’re mad!”

“Not mad, I assure you,” the Director stepped forward with a wolfish smile on his face. The smell of make-up hit me hard. Of course. No one was naturally that shade of orange. A bead of sweat trickled down the side of his face. He wiped it away casually with a white handkerchief. A smear of make-up came away with it, revealing dark grey skin underneath. “You see, we’re nearly ready. It’s a shame you won’t be around to see our glorious ascent after so long in the shadows, but there we are.”

“What are you?” I couldn’t identify his species under his heavy cologne. My stomach tightened.

He smiled horribly, and then reached to his mouth, “I suppose you might as well know before you die.” He removed a set of false teeth, revealing smaller sharper ones underneath. He swiped off the rest of his make up with his handkerchief and pushed his hair back, releasing ears which sprang out to the side. Grey skin. Sharp teeth. Pointy ears. The hairs on my arms bristled upwards and I fought to stay in control as my shifter form yearned to break free.

“Dark elf!”

“We prefer to be called Mostrim, and we’ve been waiting. Banished for thousands of years, watching from afar. Now we’re ready. It’s so sad you won’t see our rise to glory,” he stepped forward and stroked my hair, “I would keep you as a pet," I snarled and jerked my head to bite his delicate hand. He pulled out of my reach and walked back to his sidekick, "but you're too troublesome to keep around. Maxi, kill her."

"What?!" Maxi blurted out.

"I need to test your loyalty. Kill her, then take your place with us in the new order. Do it!"

"With what?"

"Her crossbow's right there…"

Maxi's eyes flicked to my weapon where he had left it on the large conference table. He edged forward to retrieve it. I stayed with my hands above my head, glaring at him. He walked quickly over to the cleaning cart where I'd left the remainder of my bolts. He selected one and loaded it. He walked back over and stood behind me. I'd trained him to shoot. He was a decent enough shot from twenty feet and now he was point blank behind my head.

"Coward," I hissed, "You could at least look me in the eyes."

He moved around in front of me. He met my gaze and held it. My eyes flicked to the bolt. Silver tipped. I braced myself for the impact. I wasn't coming back from this.

Chapter 20

I watched his finger tense on the trigger. Vass and the Director were already smiling behind him. Maxi gave me a wink and turned. He loosed the bolt into the Director's stomach and then stepped to one side. Vass fired his own crossbow. I heard the bolt sink into Maxi's muscle. He fell to the ground. In a fluid movement, I shifted and sprang at Vass. My claws sank through his suit and deep into his flesh.

"Jones…" he managed weakly before passing out.

I felt the crackle of magic make my fur stand on end. I used his chest as a springboard and pounced at the Director. He aimed a bolt of magic at me. I twisted in midair. His dark red magic grazed my side in a shock of pain. I had the sensation of ancient blood, metal and dark forests. I narrowed my eyes as I landed. The Director lunged forward. He grabbed his own portal box and activated it. Through the gateway, I glimpsed swirling colours and a strange landscape. A fae realm. I leapt as he stepped through. Too late. The portal disappeared and I hit the wall.

I shifted back into my human form, shaking my head from the impact and confronted Maxi.

"What the hell was that?!"

He winced, "Sorry…"

I glared at him then gave him a hug, "Thanks for saving my life."

He gave me a lopsided grin then grimaced. I looked at the bolt embedded deep in his arm. I located my handbag where it had fallen from the cleaning trolley and fished around inside. My questing hand found what I was looking for. A bottle of *Madam Mim's Cure All*. Not much left. I opened it and offered it to him. He took a swig and pulled a face at the strong taste of aniseed and whisky.

I surveyed the room, "What a mess…" There was only one thing to do. I pulled up Gwen's details on my phone and dialled. The screen informed me there was no signal down here in the basement. I looked around and spotted a landline on the table. I picked my way over the gutted werewolf and dialled her number.

By the time she arrived less than fifteen minutes later, I had checked which of the fallen supernaturals would survive and had tied up those who were already beginning to regain consciousness.

Gwen gave a low whistle as she entered the room with Dot in tow, "Another mess for me to clean up Jones?"

"What would your life be like without me?"

"Peaceful?"

"Boring."

She laughed. Her eyes raked the room and she called in her fae medic. It was the same young woman who had patched me up. She gave me a nod and rushed to the most obviously injured creature: the werewolf sprawled on the floor. She pulled on rubber gloves and began stuffing his guts back inside his stomach. I didn't envy her that job. I watched as she picked a bit of carpet fluff of his entrails and shuddered.

Dot was bending over Vass, "What the dzrak?"

"Turns out he was part of an evil cult with our Director," I nudged his leg with my high-heel.

"This looks bad."

"Don't worry, I've got proof," I rummaged in my bag and pulled out a Dictaphone. I rewound it and played her an excerpt of our conversation. It was muffled but clear enough thanks to Maxi's enhancements. Both the vampire's and the harpy's eyes widened in shock. Then Gwen recovered and held out her clawed hand. I shook my head, "I'll turn it in once I've made copies."

"Paranoid much?"

"Wouldn't you be? He set those idiots who nearly killed Dick on me."

"Bastard."

I nodded in agreement. There wasn't much more to say. I stayed until the medic had seen to Maxi's wound. He was healing well thanks to her magic and the *Cure All* and insisted on walking out without any support. I offered him and Dot a lift back. Dot shook her head saying she was staying overnight with a friend but Maxi accepted. Outside, I spotted a familiar car parked on the street, right next to a no parking sign. Dick was having an animated conversation with an elderly traffic warden who was writing a ticket. I rubbed the back of my neck and strode over.

"Is there a problem here?"

He looked me over, taking in the bloodstains on my smart suit. To his credit, he merely swallowed before regaining his confidence and waving his ticket book in my direction. London traffic duty must be hardcore. "Who are you love?"

"The owner of the vehicle."

"Then we've got a problem. See that no parking sign? It means no parking!"

"It's on official business," I flashed him my Magical Liaison Office ID.

He shrugged, "Sorry love, it's already written up. You're lucky I didn't call a tow truck. Now move it!" He thrust a flimsy yellow strip of paper at me and stalked off. I took it without looking and turned my attention to Dick.

"What are you doing here? I thought you were going to wait at the hotel?" I gestured for Dick to scoot into the passenger seat. He started to protest then gave in as I took off my stained jacket and shoved it into the car.

"I thought you might need back up," he mumbled.

"What were you going to do? Get another ticket?"

"I don't know, I just…wanted to be here."

I sighed and gave him a smile to let him know I wasn't really upset. I waited for Maxi to climb in, then I started the car. I revved the engine to see if I could make the traffic warden jump. He took out his pad of tickets again and waved it at me. I got the impression he'd rather be giving me the finger, but he was in uniform. I waved back and drove off carefully. I didn't need another fine tonight.

We dropped Maxi off outside his apartment building or 'London residence' as he called it. It was in a flashy part of town that reminded me he came from money. He wasn't going to be roughing it in a postage stamp sized flat share.

Maxi stopped at the kerb and turned back to the car, "Well, er, bye. I guess I'll see you on Monday, yah?"

I sat back in my seat. It hadn't occurred to me that I didn't have to go back to my old house. "Yeah," I responded with a wave. A doorman in a burgundy uniform opened the door for him as he called goodbye and headed in. I shook my head. We ran in very different worlds. I clenched my jaw. Just days ago, I would have jumped at the chance to get back to work and forget about my home again, but now…I glanced across at the author gazing out of the window of my car.

"So, I guess I'm not on sabbatical anymore…"

"Sure. You'll be wanting to get back to the day job…"

"You can stay, at the house I mean. If you want."

He nodded then surprised me by gripping my hand before pressing it to his hot lips, "I'd rather stay with you." My stomach did a weird flip as warmth flooded me.

I turned the car around and headed across the city to the hotel. Dick's sat nav on his phone called out directions and, apart from trying to take us the wrong way down a one-way street, got us there with minimal issues. The heavily-rouged receptionist gave me a long look as she signed us in. I had changed quickly into some clean clothes but my skin still had flecks of blood on it. I was beginning to wonder if I'd gone overboard with the werewolf.

I flashed my ID again and mentioned something about a company paintball event. She didn't look convinced but she handed us the keycards like a consummate professional.

I took Dick's hand and led the way to our room. I swiped the key card and pushed open the door. Once inside, I turned and pressed myself against him, giving him a lingering kiss. I gestured to the king-sized bed. "Why don't you get comfortable and I'll get cleaned up?"

I stripped off and headed for the shower. It took longer than I'd expected to get all the gore off my body and out of my hair. I cursed the inadequately sized tiny bottles of shampoo as I emptied both of them trying to get clean. Eventually I was done. I dried myself and took a minute to make sure I looked good in the mirror. I mussed up my sleek black hair to give it a sexy look then stepped out of the bathroom.

Dick was asleep on top of the covers. Figures. I grabbed a robe from behind the door, turned off the lights and snuggled into bed beside him. Maybe I could take some real time away from work.

Epilogue

I was standing outside the small guest house, sipping a cup of coffee, as my thoughts drifted to the events in Breconia. The dragon egg had been restored to its parents and I had congratulated the team on a successful case closed before escaping to my weekend retreat for a well-earned break. I promised myself I would relax this time. I focused on the farm house. The roof was finished and we'd be able to move inside soon. I still had to decide what I wanted to keep from Mum's things and I wasn't looking forward to that job, but it would be good to finally move on now that I was accepting that piece of my past rather than running from it.

It was then that I noticed the golden dot in the sky. Dick appeared behind me and slipped his arms around my waist. He nibbled at my neck. I leaned against him. My eyes closed momentarily as I gave into the pleasure. I felt his lips curve into a smile against my skin. A squawking cry called overhead. I ignored it and turned in his embrace. I didn't know when I'd next be able to escape work and come here and I didn't want anything to ruin our brief time together. Plus I'd promised myself I'd relax. That meant no work stuff while I was on holiday. The harsh squawk came again. I swear if Gwen was playing a prank on me…Reluctantly, I pulled myself away and looked up.

A gryphgeon circled above us. Its golden feathers and fur caught the sunlight making it seem like living gold. The cat-sized official elven messenger did another loop before swooping down and dropping a piece of card. It landed on the cast iron bannister leading down from the steps in front of us, all four of its feet gripping the railing. It appraised me with its orange eyes, the hooked beak only just managing to make it look less like a pigeon.

"What on earth is that?"

I sighed, "A gryphgeon. The official messengers of the elven court. Think of it like a cross between a cat and a pigeon."

Dick reached out his hand to stroke the small creature's head. I placed my own hand on his, "I wouldn't. They're very proud and it could give you a nasty peck."

Dick looked at the cat-sized bird dubiously, but he withdrew his hand and rested it in the pocket of his faded jeans. The messenger twisted its head to peck at a spot just beneath its wing joints, about where the feathers turned into sleek fur.

I bent and retrieved the thick card. Swirling vines patterned the edges in gold leaf. The symbol of the Elven High Council was stamped on one side: a tree with a crown looped around the trunk. I flipped it over. There was an ivy leaf stamped at the top and golden writing in copperplate font. I read the message:

Agent Ruth Jones is cordially invited to the annual Equinox Ball on the Twenty Second of September.

RSVP

"What does it say?"

"Just an invitation."

"It looks fancy, are you going to go?"

I turned back to him and looped my hands around his neck, "It's the weekend before I'm due to go back into the Office, I thought we could stay in."

I let the invitation drop from my hand and sunk myself into his kiss. The gryphgeon would have to take back a no from me. After all, I'd already saved the Magical Liaison Office from a dark elf infiltration, what else could happen this year?

Here's a couple of bonus chapters that show Agent Jones' view of the events at the end of Solstice of Dragons – Book 2 in the Rise of Dragons Series.

Bonus Chapter 1

Goosebumps rose on my skin. Magic thrummed in the air from the Summer Solstice celebrations within the circle of Stonehenge. I checked my watch. Nearly sunrise. Then we could clear these people out and complete our mission.

My ears pricked. A low rumble sounded from the speakers behind me. Odd, I hadn't expected them to be turned on yet. The sound made me uncomfortable. I shrugged that off. Instead I glared at the members of the crowd who were looking at our small group, annoyed at the interruption to their festivities. The sky began to turn a pinky colour as the sun started its rise on this celebrated day in the magical calendar.

The volume behind me increased. I frowned, annoyed that I had sent Maxi to the third point. He would know what to do about the speakers. I pulled out my phone to call him and swore softly. No signal. The magical energy from the crowd must be blocking the mobile signal. I took a couple of steps away from the henge. My phone rang in my hands. I answered gruffly.

"What?"

Lorandir's elven voice sounded brokenly through the phone, "Our speaker's making weird sounds. Should we have started clearing the crowd?"

"No, not yet. Let them enjoy the sunrise, then we'll get them out of here."

"There's something else. We heard something…underground."

The ground began to rumble beneath my feet. I accidently hung up as I stared at the grass shaking slightly. Schiztz. What was going on? I strained my own keen ears. Another sound seemed to reply to the noise from the speakers. From beneath the ground. I considered shifting into my lynx form to hear better. That's when I noticed three figures pushing through the crowd towards us.

I caught Dot's eye and widened my legs into a standard security pose. She mimicked me and fingered her standard issue crossbow. The figures paused at the edge of the crowd, staring directly at us.

"Return to your celebrations please," I used my authoritative voice, projecting it loudly over the few feet between us.

One of them smiled nastily in the pre-dawn light and lifted his hands. I clocked the floor length robes. Deep red. That was never good. Brown ropes snaked from his hands towards Dot. She disappeared into a blur, dodging them easily.

"Vampire! Watch your necks!" I heard one of the figures shout in warning.

I used the distraction to fire my crossbow at the nearest sorcerer. The sorcerer raised a magical shield to block the bolt headed for his chest. While he was focusing on magic, I ran. Shifting into my lynx form, I zigzagged around his shield and leapt. He staggered under my weight. I dug my claws in. I felt the fabric rip. He cried out. I dug deeper into his flesh. His eyes fluttered shut. Light weight. Confident he was out, I turned my attention to the other two. Dot's speed was keeping them busy but I saw one start to murmur an incantation. That was never good. I snarled and used his friend's body as a springboard, forcing myself off with force. The robed figure heard me coming and shifted his attention to me. I twisted in the air, dodging the bolt of magic. I felt the force of it whistle overhead. Another bolt hit my foreleg with a fiery burst. I roared in pain and anger and powered through. I landed hard on my three uninjured legs. Nearly there. I feinted right. He took the bait and fired off another blast of magic followed by more brownish ropes where he thought I was going to be. I cannoned into his legs with a snarl. I raked my claws deep into his thigh. He summoned up another spell. I clamped my teeth hard onto his hand. His cry of pain interrupted the incantation. Troll blood filled my mouth. I spat it out as best I could. Other members of the crowd were staring at us. I felt a crackle of magic from the other side of the henge.

"Solstice is sacred!" boomed a voice from the same direction. The same direction that Lorandir and Amethyst were in. I turned my head to see if my supernatural senses could pick up anything. The troll used my distraction to pull a cruel, serrated knife. I caught his movement just in time and twisted out of the way. It was a desperate stab. I leapt and my claws ripped through his shoulder. He rolled to the floor. I felt the bloodlust rise. The urge to finish him off. I fought it back. The bitter taste of troll blood was already making me gag. I didn't want any more of that. Besides, we'd need to question them. Do things by the book. I glanced over to where Dot was leaning over her assailant. She was tying him up with his own conjured ropes. I nodded. Very neat.

He rolled suddenly and thrust upwards. A sharp knife glinted towards Dot. I bunched my muscles, grunting at the pain in my injured leg, springing forward. Green magic arced from the crowd towards us. I was forced to the ground. The robed attacker struggled against the crackling magic as it pushed his hand back to the floor. Dot was down too. What the dzrak? The magic stayed, pinning us down for a few seconds. Then it was gone. Dot recovered first and delivered a swift punch to the man on the floor, knocking him out. I got to my feet and looked around. I couldn't see who had cast that powerful magic. Ropes snaked out of mid-air and bound the robed figures tightly. Dzraking wizards. Dzraking Stonehenge. Dzraking Solstice. I snarled in frustration at someone doing my job for me.

I padded back to the speaker and sat on my haunches, considering. Could I really hear anything underground or was it a trick of the vibrations? The single stone set in front of the standing circle of Stonehenge began to glow pinkly as it caught the light of the sunrise. Dot joined me after binding the other two with the ropes. I admired her deft fingers as they work and wondered where she had learned to tie knots like that.

Light footsteps approached. I turned. The elf, Lorandir, was racing towards us. His elven speed and soft tread meant he had nearly reached us before I'd clocked him. Amethyst, the shorter half-dwarf in need of some cardio training, was running behind him.

He stopped and began talking. Barely out of breath. Amethyst panted as she arrived alongside him, her small wyrm pet in tow, and took in the figures on the ground. I watched her turn and stare at the speaker as Lorandir was filling us in on the sounds they'd heard. She handed her wrym to her gnomish friend, Aloora. She hefted her large double-headed axe and destroyed the electronic equipment with one blow. Her technique was shoddy but effective.

"No!" Maxi cried out. He fell to his knees and cradled the broken pieces of the speaker. I knew he loved his gadgets, but this seemed excessive.

Amethyst took out some energy on the largest remaining piece of the speaker. I watched her slam the axe into the broken device again and again. I let it pass. Sometimes we all needed to let off some steam. She leant on her axe after she'd finished, panting hard at the exertion.

"What?"

I shifted back to my human form, "Right, now that Amethyst has got her anger issues out. We need to cut out the other speaker. Maxi, Dot, disconnect it." They raced off. Dot blurred slightly as she used her vampiric speed.

"Did you make anything out while you were listening?"

“No. But you’re a shifter? How…?”

I ignored Amethyst and turned up the force of my glare. The elf replied. “It might have been words but I didn’t understand the language.”

“Aloora, you’re the language expert. Get rid of that wyrm and get your ear to the ground. Lorandir, tell her any sounds you heard.”

I felt rather than heard Madam Mim approaching with an elderly man sporting a close cut beard and a druidic robe. He carried a twisted staff in one hand like a weapon. Merlin. I nodded to them both.

“It is worse than we feared,” Madam Mim spoke grimly without preamble. “I can feel the energies shifting, we don’t have long.”

“Can you contain it?” I was blunt.

“I don’t know, but we will do our best.”

I nodded in reply and the two figures stood either side of the smaller standing stone directly aligned with the sunrise and raised their arms, gathering magic to them. I watched, narrowing my eyes.

“What’s going on? Who’s he? What are they going to do? How are you a shifter? What is happening?” Amethyst interrupted my thoughts.

I rubbed the back of my neck, trying to weigh up how much to tell her. I sighed. She had as much right to know the truth as anyone. “It looks like someone’s trying to waken the dragon we think is underneath Stonehenge. Merlin and Mim are going to try to use their magic to put the dragon back to sleep. I'm a shifter in the normal way, but you can't sense me because of this." I pointed to my wrist and the gold band with a lynx's head carved into it. The magical dampener that let me pass for human to those with magical senses, including the steampunk style goggles the half-dwarf favoured.

"Merlin and Mim?"

I nodded, glad we weren't going to focus on my being a shifter. I turned my attention to the magic users, who now had green and blue light streaming from their hands as they cast their spells. Their hair and clothing whirled around them in their vortex of power. The stone circle was now empty of all bar the last stragglers, who were clamouring to get out of the area.

A magical field settled over the stone circle. It was suddenly strangely silent after the racket of the Solstice celebrations. Even the birds were quiet, their dawn chorus stopped out of respect for, or fear of, the magic expended.

I stopped tapping my foot in the silence and settled for glaring at the gnome and elf stretched out on the ground. Amethyst's small wyrm growled on her shoulder. I narrowed my eyes at it. Aloora finally lifted herself up from the ground and walked over.

She shrugged apologetically. "I think there are words there but no one has heard Draconic spoken by dragons themselves in millennia. I'm relying on Lorandir's interpretations of the sounds and Draconic is a contextual language…I'd only be guessing."

“Well what’s your best guess?” I pinched the bridge of her nose in frustration. I needed my employees to get answers not guesswork.

“My best guess is that it’s not good. The rumbling is getting stronger and I think it’s awake and confused.”

The wyrm was bobbing up and down now, alternately whining and blowing small flickers of flame at the henge. “Er, I think Errol agrees with your guess. He’s pretty agitated,” Amethyst chimed in.

I turned and narrowed my eyes at the wyrm. I stepped closer and held out my hand. He sniffed it but continued to look over my shoulder to where Mim and Merlin were standing.

Dot materialised at my side in a blur of speed. “Speaker destroyed.” I nodded. I could trust her to handle things.

Errol let out an anguished roar. Amethyst swore and I resisted clutching my own sensitive ears. The ground shook. I planted my feet widely, trusting my reflexes to keep me standing. The half-dwarf looked like she was having trouble keeping her footing.

Mim and Merlin swayed slightly, still pouring magic into the stone circle. The shaking stopped. Then the ground reverberated forcefully. The two magic users staggered backwards as they were forced out of the circle.

Amethyst ran over to help them get clear of the stones, I was close behind her.

“We can’t hold it,” Mim breathed.

The stones began to tremble, the magic field dissipating as the force from beneath the ground increased. The monoliths quaked as the ground imploded. The earth crumbled down and a gaping hole appeared. I jumped to avoid the opening.

There was a sighing sound as if the planet itself was holding its breath and then, slowly, swaying slightly and blinking in the dawn light, a huge crested head appeared. Its pale white scales reflected the light, making it seem like it was the embodiment of the Solstice sun.

It opened its huge jaws, threw its head back and roared to the sky. I scrunched my face at the force of the roar on my keen ears. Its clawed front feet gripped the edge of the hole and it slithered upwards out of the ground. Once out in the open, its true scale was enormous. I craned my neck upwards to try to take it all in. Its long tail still trailed into the dark cavern. I knew a predator when I saw one and every instinct was telling me I was on the bottom of the food chain here. It beat its wings several times. My nose twitched. The smell of it reminded me of the wreckage of Cardiff Castle after the first dragon was awoken, but different. It reminded me of the crocodiles at a zoo I had visited once. Crocodiles crossed with snow and something else, something ancient.

"The white dragon has risen." Merlin spoke in a strained voice. The hairs on my arms stood on end as Merlin gathered power to him and a blast of magical lightning shot from his hands towards the creature. The dragon roared again as the bolt of magic connected with its chest.

It flapped its large wings and took flight, gusts of wind hitting us with each down stroke. The temperature cooled. Suddenly, instead of the growing heat of a summer's day, the smell of the air changed. It felt like a crisp winter's morning. I shivered and considered shifting to stay warm under my thick layer of fur. I took a deep breath and a second to assess things. Something was off. I hadn't been present when the first dragon was unleashed upon the world but I'd seen and smelled the aftermath. It had been…destructive.

As it hovered above us, its jewelled green eyes alit on Merlin with hatred and it opened its mouth and breathed ice directly at him. An ice dragon! I hadn't even known such things existed. Amethyst was already in front of the ancient mage with the shield from her axe's rune activated. The icy blast buffeted the shield.

"Move!" she yelled. The magician staggered away.

The shield gave way and the half-dwarf was encased in ice. The gnome yelled something guttural. Everyone ignored her. I caught the flicker of flame inside the icy tomb.

"This wasn't supposed to happen!" Maxi wailed.

I wanted to shake him, "What?!"

"The speakers, they weren't meant to do this!"

I felt my teeth lengthening as I fought to control my anger. "You did this?"

His eyes boggled in fear as he took in our frozen teammate, the huge dragon floating above us and my temper. I turned away before I did something I would regret. Enough watching. Time to take charge.

“You!” I pointed to Aloora, the newest member of my team and the least trained in combat, “take his sword and guard Maxi! Film everything! We’re going to need it for evidence,” I muttered. I narrowed my eyes at Maxi and raised my voice again, “I’ll deal with you later! Don’t cause any trouble!” Maxi surrendered his enchanted sword and they raced off to hide behind one of the large stones.

“Get her out of there!” The rest of the team responded to my order. Dot was there first with her sword. She spoke the Dwarfish word for fire and pressed the blade to the thick ice.

I focused on the dragon. I cried out. Its vision focused on me. I lifted my crossbow and shot a bolt directly at one of its jewel-green eyes. I didn’t have time to reload as it drew breath. I leapt to one side and shifted as it let loose another blast. In my lynx form, I dodged and dived, keeping its focus. Mim and Merlin saw what I was trying to do from where they were sheltered behind one of the, now leaning, stones. They let off their own bolts of magic at its thick, pale hide. It roared in annoyance. Good. Keep it distracted. I saw the elf standing there, trying feebly to help free Amethyst. Irritated, I shifted back.

“Lorandir! I need your speed.”

His keen ears heard me, but he still looked undecided. I didn’t have time for this. The dragon shot out acid green poison from its mouth. Great. I leapt to one side but the splashback hit my tail. I let out a cat-like growl of annoyance. I expected the dragon to press its attack. Instead it turned and shot off another poison blast towards one of the large lintels. I saw the elf leap off it and respond with his own blast of magic. Finally.

We wove right and left, distracting the creature. I dodged an icy blast then sprung up to claw at its shoulder. Its scales were hard armour. I couldn't get any purchase and slid down. It raked its talons over its body, trying to get rid of me. I used its leg as a springboard and pounced away. I immediately leapt again to avoid its stamping feet. Close combat wasn't going to work with this enemy. A bolt of magic to its jaw caused it to turn sharply. I was forgotten for now.

The smell of magical flames stung my nostrils. An ear-splitting roar came from the dragon. It whirled around and I saw a burn mark on its scaly tail. Dot blurred into vision at my side, her enchanted sword burning brightly. The dragon rushed upwards, beating its wings strongly to get away. The downdraught rippled across my fur. I risked a glance over at the icy cave. The half-dwarf was free. Good. Now to try to get us out of this without any major casualties.

The dragon narrowed its eyes at the cause of its minor injury and sent a blast of ice towards Dot. I dived to the side. She jumped and rolled, avoiding the main impact. I heard her sharp intake of breath and smelt the metallic tang of blood. One of the icy crystals had pierced her leg.

Rumbling thrummed up my legs. I tensed to keep my footing even in lynx form. The others were struggling as the vibrations grew. I heard Amethyst's exclamation.

"What the dzrak?"

I tilted my head. There seemed to be a rhythm behind the vibrations. A pounding, thumping noise that shook the ground every second or so. Footsteps. Of a large creature.

Another dragon's head, smaller this time, peeped from the cavernous hole in the ground. It gave a small barking noise followed by a chirp. The larger dragon swooped down and perched on the edge of the hole. I leapt slightly, in time with its landing to avoid the jolt that sent the others staggering.

I heard a creak. One of the larger upright stones started to tilt precariously. Lorandir was in its path, his back to the danger as he stared at the dragon. I raced forward to push him out of the way. Amethyst got there first. She launched herself towards the stone and stood between it and the elf. She raised her hands as if she could stop it from falling. I watched it in slow motion as I ran to try to save them both.

My fur stood on end as power coursed around the half-dwarf. Purple light pulsed from the axe she still held. The rock stayed leaning at an impossible angle above her. I slowed, instinctively not wanting to get close to that power. It smelled earthy and old. My eyes widened as the stone ground back into an upright position, reversing its fall. Oblivious to us, Amethyst patted the standing stone before turning. She began to blush as she realised we were all staring at her. Even the dragons were looking at her curiously. She raised her hand towards them. What the dzrak was she doing?

The large dragon took flight again with a shriek and the smaller one followed it. Great. They had interpreted her as a threat. They dived in tandem and delivered short icy blasts across the field, turning their heads from left to right as they peppered the ground with ice crystals. I ducked and dived as I avoided the rain of ice. I heard a cry of pain. Amethyst had been hit.

I tried to think. The large dragon stopped its attack suddenly, hovering above us. The smaller one did a loop around it and beat its wings to stay close to its side. Both creatures turned their heads in a westerly direction, ignoring us all. I strained to hear what had distracted them. Not even my excellent hearing could make it out.

The large dragon made a strange sound, a cross between a growl and a croon, then it beat its wings strongly and flew west, away from the morning sun. The smaller dragon flying in its wake. We watched the creatures as they climbed, quickly gaining altitude. They flew out of sight rapidly, glinting gold as their pale scales reflected the light.

The summer's heat hit me as quickly as it had left, promising to be another scorching hot day. I padded around the crystals that were already starting to melt now they were out of range of the white dragon. The crisp smell of snow left my nose, replaced by cut grass, meadow flowers and blood.

I approached the elf and half-dwarf. He was healing her. I could feel the crackle of nature-like elven magic from her as the greenish golden glow of his magic enveloped her arm. His face was full of tenderness and concern. A soft, sappy look played over her features. Ugh I didn't need lovebirds when we had dragons to worry about.

I shifted back to my human form and turned my gaze upwards in the direction the dragons had flown. A mystery for later. I swept an appraising eye over the chaos left of Stonehenge and the cringing captives still on the ground. One of them was still. Great. Looks like there was a casualty after all. I pinched the bridge of my nose and let out a long sigh. At least it wasn't one of my team.

“Right. Let’s wrap this up.” I strode over to where Aloora was putting her smartphone away and trying to look menacing as Maxi’s guard. I narrowed my eyes, feeling my pupils narrowed into slits as I tried to control my anger.

Maxi was hugging his legs to his body muttering, “It wasn’t supposed to happen,” over and over again with a wild look in his eyes.

“I’ll deal with you later.” I dismissed Maxi and pulled out my phone. I walked around the wreckage of Stonehenge, assessing the damage. I had to do something while we waited for the clean-up team and I needed the thinking time.

Within fifteen minutes, a van had pulled up directly at the gates of Stonehenge and several muscled Magical Liaison Officers were sprinting into the field. I greeted them and pointed out our attackers. They must have felt the magical disturbance caused by the dragons. I could sense their magical gear as they grabbed the cultists and roughly marched them to the van at crossbow point.

Bonus Chapter 2

Back in the van, I drove us back. My injured arm was already beginning to heal thanks to my shifter magic.

Dot was sitting next to Maxi in the back, hand on her sword and looking grim. Maxi himself looked awful. His mad professor style hair was even more dishevelled and he gazed despondently out of the window at the fields rolling past.

Madam Mim was sitting next to me. A slight frown played over her brow. It worried me, I'd never seen her as anything other than slightly amused with the world. I clenched my jaw, still trying to think. I pulled up at Avebury, outside her cottage and noticed people running in the road.

I leapt out of the car and grabbed a woman dressed in a flowing skirt.

"What's going on?"

The rest of the team piled out behind me.

“The ground, it was shaking…the stones…” I let go of the terrified woman and sprinted towards the stone circle. The elf was at my side almost instantly, a grim look on his handsome face.

The field was empty of people and several stones had fallen over. I surveyed the scene. A small mound of fresh earth pushed up through the grass. I sniffed. Earth, ice and that crocodilian smell again. Dragons.

“Hey, this is weir…” I turned as Amethyst fell through the ground and landed hard in a deep, underground cavern.

I pinched the bridge of my nose again. That girl attracted accidents. “Are you alright down there?”

She stared up at me from the earthy floor. “Just peachy!” she wheezed.

I stifled a smile. “We’re getting a rope.”

I didn’t wait for a reply and sprinted off to retrieve a rope from the van. Dot was recovering too but her speed was impaired by her leg wound and she needed sleep not sunlight to heal.

“Keep her talking in case she’s injured,” I shouted over my shoulder to Aloora.

I let the rope down through the hole and heard it coil onto the floor.

“I can’t climb that!”

I sighed. I really needed to insist on basic fitness and combat training before accepting people into any taskforces. I pulled up the rope and dug in my mock crocodile skin handbag I had grabbed for a harness. I secured it then dropped the rope back into the cavern. "Pull twice when you're ready and we'll pull you up."

I felt two sharp pulls on the rope and nodded to the team. We hoisted her upwards. I grunted slightly at the weight. Finally, her head crested the opening. I nodded to the elf to pull her up. She grunted in pain as she bumped onto the ground.

As he healed her – again – I pulled some warning cones and tape from my bag and set them up round the hole. I was glad I had had that bag bespelled so it could carry anything without weighing a tonne. I waved the team away and made another call. The clean-up teams at the Magical Liaison Office were going to have a busy day.

I waited for them on my own. I needed time to think. Someone had used the Office's speakers to wake the dragons here. Someone who knew what our taskforce was doing. I didn't like where this was taking me. Maxi. He was the obvious answer. But…we'd worked together for years. I got on with him better than anyone. He'd even put in for a transfer shortly after I'd been made head of the Wales branch so we could continue working together. He knew every handbook inside and out. He was more committed to the Office code of keeping magical and mundane beings living in peace that anyone. Could he really want to betray that code? Was he really a traitor? Something didn't add up.

A non-descript black van pulled up and I watched as the clean-up squad poured out.

"Hi Gwen."

"You've made a real mess here. Second one today so they told me."

"I get all the good gigs."

She smiled at me, then turned to her team, "I'll put in the calls to the press. Do what you can to patch this place up. It's a heritage site, so I want it exactly like it was."

"There's a hole in the ground!"

"They teach you those observation skills at university did they? I can see there's a bloody hole in the ground. Figure out how we fix it or failing that, make it look like there was a bloody gas explosion. Get moving before it gets even hotter out here!" Her grey wings unfurled to emphasise her annoyance. I smiled as her team backed away. The harpy could be terrifying when she was riled.

"I'll leave you to it then," I liked her efficiency and no-nonsense approach. Gwendoline waved me away in acknowledgement, tucking her clawed wings back against her back neatly as she shouted orders to her team.

Thank you for reading book three in the Rise of Dragons series. If you enjoyed this book, you can get a free prequel to my Rise of Dragons series by signing up to my mailing list on www.gemmaclatworthy.com. And join the conversation at Gemma's book wyrms or see all my books before they're published on patreon.com /G_Clatworthy.

As an independent author, your reviews help me decide which series to keep going so please do leave one for Darkest Deception and if you enjoyed this book, try Attack on Avalon, book five in the Rise of Dragons series.

Books in the Rise of Dragons series:

Awakening

Solstice of Dragons

Equinox Betrayal

Darkest Deception

Attack on Avalon

Fated Bloodlines

About the Author

Gemma started writing during the 2020 lockdown and loves fantasy fiction and dragons in particular. She lives in Wiltshire with her family and two cats and also enjoys crafts of all kinds. You can see all her writing on patreon.com/G_Clatworthy. Join the conversation at Gemma's book wyrms readers' group on Facebook.

She also writes children's books. You can find out more on her website www.gemmaclatworthy.com or follow her on Instagram (www.instagram.com/gemmaclatworthy) or Facebook (www.facebook.com/gemmaclatworthy).

www.ingramcontent.com/pod-product-compliance
Ingram Content Group UK Ltd.
Pitfield, Milton Keynes, MK11 3LW, UK
UKHW040006200726
13854UKWH00001B/61